The

Gray House

Present Day

Maybe now there will be peace. Not only for myself, but also for the many others, living and nonliving, that have had their lives altered by this dwelling.

I was beginning to think this day would never come, I think to myself over the rumble of bulldozers and dump trucks that reverberate down the busy street.

Peering at the immense gray shell in front of me, a shiver runs down my spine. If this is supposed to bring me peace, then why do I feel so apprehensive?

The rumble of the first bulldozer is deafening as the bucket raises and takes a chunk of the decrepit roof. The hundreds of pigeons, that have made nests throughout the plaster covered wood lath walls, fly out in flocks.

As hard as I try not to glance at the tiny window above the front porch, my eyes deceive me and shift anyways. In that tiny window, Abby stands alone, in the familiar dirty and ripped white dress. Just as I somehow knew she would be. The scared and sad expression that she usually wears on her child-like face has been replaced with something dark. The blackened eyes and grin that has preempted the once was angel face, let's me know that *he* is here. *He* will always be here.

I despise this place and just about everything associated with it.

As the second bulldozer lifts towards the roof of the attached barn, the long-standing wood crumbles, leaving behind a cloud of dust.

Amongst the pile of ruins, something catches my eye, it's a blue and gray Power Wheel motorcycle that once belonged to my brother. Long forgotten memories of the day we moved in flood my thoughts.

Chapter One

"You know, back when your Aunt Karen was in high school, we lived in this same house with your Uncle Alan." Gram says in a cheery, yet raspy voice. I roll my eyes. I know my Grandparents are trying to find some sort of light during this dark time, but I just don't want to move.

This is the second time we have moved. The last time was eleven years ago and being only two years old, I don't remember much. Just that my dad never used boxes like most of my friend's parents seemed to when they moved. Black trash bags, a pickup truck and a few extra hands was all he needed. That is still true today. The back of his dark green Ford is loaded up with black bags and random junk, as Dad and Grandpa would call it. Not Gram though, nothing is junk to her. And that's probably why we have taken so many trips from my childhood home, all the way across town to this freshly painted blueish gray house.

Standing in the driveway, alongside the busy road, this old house looks huge. There's so many windows, ten just on the front side. One in particular, above the porch, catches my attention. Unlike the other nine, this one is smaller and by looking at the wooden frame, I'm not sure how or if it would even open. I bet it gets pretty stuffy in that room. The view wouldn't be all that spectacular either.

"That's my old train room." Uncle Alan startles me, and I try not to let it show. He gets a kick out of scaring people. By people, I mean me. When I was around five, everyone had me convinced that he was Joe Beef. And I'm not talking about the Wikipedia definition; Charles McKiernan, well-known Irish-Canadian Montreal tavern owner, innkeeper and philanthropist. No, this Joe Beef was the scariest thing one could ever think of. He lived in the dark, and was somehow, everywhere all the time. Now that I'm older, I'm pretty sure that Uncle Alan made him up. Afterall, he does watch far too many horror movies. Even so, I'm still afraid of what's lurking in the dark.

"Train room?" The room doesn't look all that big from down here. "How do you get up there? I must have missed the stairs." Mentally, I tour the house again. If there were stairs, I'm certain I would have remembered.

"They are in the hallway by your fathers' room. Just on the other side of that door over there." My eyes follow towards the other end of the house, stopping at a door I didn't see until now. "The new owners have since covered it with drywall. I'm not sure why though. A little drywall won't keep *them* up there." I wait for his one-of-a-kind boisterous laugh, but when he doesn't laugh, I feel my throat tighten.

"Alan, knock it off." My dad looks angry. It's been an exhausting day, but I have a feeling this attitude has something to do with whatever Uncle Alan was about to tell me. Now I'm intrigued. "Emma, why don't you and Marie see if your gram or Aunt Susanne need help with dinner?"

"Okay." Since my Gram's health has depleted over the last few years, everyone helps out as much as they can. Sometimes, this just frustrates her more because there are certain ways, she wants things done. *If you want something done right, do it yourself.* Is one of her many mottos.

In the kitchen the fresh paint smell is being replaced by greasy hamburgers and previously frozen french fries. Just as I figured, Gram and Aunt Susanne have dinner under control. Since I was only two the last time we moved, I don't know what we ate while moving. I do know that I can't wait to eat some real food and not all this premade frozen garbage.

"Want to help me unpack my room?" I ask Marie and she just nods, causing her brown curly hair to bounce. I've always been jealous of her curls. My fine, straight hair has just one random wave to it. I've tried to curl it but within twenty minutes, it's flat again. Just like she's always straightening hers, but as soon as it gets wet, it springs up like a slinky. We've always wished we could trade hair, even if just for a day.

Marie closes my new bedroom door and smiles. "My dad has told me stories from when he used to live here. This place is haunted, you know."

I glance around the room. The white walls and gray painted wood floors don't give off a creepy vibe. However, the rectangle vent in the ceiling is creepy. "I'm sure it is, most old places are." I half joke but deep down I sense something is off. I can feel goosebumps forming on my arms. *She's just trying to scare me, just like her dad does.* I tell myself over and over.

"Did Grammy tell you any of the stories? Like the time Little Alan was found playing in the road? When my mom asked him why, he told her that his imaginary friend that lived inside his Tonka truck told him to. After that, my dad put it inside the dumbwaiter in the kitchen, on the very top shelf."

Kids say stuff like that all the time so that they don't get in trouble. Marie seems to be enjoying this, so I try not to burst her bubble. "That's weird."

"Right? Or how about the time my dad was in his train room, and something lifted him off the ground and pinned him against the wall? That's scary! I don't think I'd be able to live here." She shakes her head before the rest of her body trembles from a cold chill.

"Well, since the upstairs has been closed off, I don't think we have anything to worry about." Right? I swallow the lump forming in my throat.

"Ghost can go through walls, Emma. Just ask Grammy."

"Grammy also thinks aliens can walk through walls." She raises her eyebrow and I know this is my chance to change the subject. I already feel creeped out enough by this house. I don't need to hear any more stories. Stories, that's all they are. Typically, stories are embellished to sound more interesting or intense. Between Marie and Uncle Alan, I think it's safe to say they are just trying to intensify the actual events to scare me. Not happening today. "Actually, she has been stressing about the oversized parking lot through the woods out back. She said it's big enough for seven UFO's."

Her hands are firm on her hips as she raises her eyebrow. "I'm telling you that you now live in a haunted house and you're comparing it to *aliens*?"

"Sure am." Lowering my voice, I lean closer and whisper, "I don't want to make any ghost that may live here mad. Like you said, *I live here now*."

"Okay, fine. But, if you change your mind, just let me know and I'll tell you more."

"I won't." Excitement drains from her brown eyes as she realizes that I honestly don't want to hear anymore. Maybe when we move out, I'll ask her. Not until then though.

Chapter Two

"Emma, come play outside with me!" My little brother Jake wines as he tugs at my arm. Times like this, I wish he had a friend his own age. It gets exhausting playing with him all day.

"Fine, but only for a little bit." Since we both ended up with a bad cold after the move, I have piles of schoolwork to catch up on. Jake's lucky to only be in elementary school, instead of eighth grade. He probably missed out on learning a few sight words, whereas I have loads of makeup work that still needs to be done.

At least it's warm outside today and the snow is almost melted. We both still have poufy winter jackets on though. Gram makes us wear them anytime the weather drops below sixty degrees.

As we make our way around the massive house, Jake points up at one of the windows on the second floor and waves. "Hi hi!" He shouts.

"Jake, who are you saying hi to? No one can get up there." I look up again, but I can't see anyone. There's a silver oval sticker on one of the windows. That must be what he sees. I guess it kind of resembles a face.

Ignoring me as usual, he keeps walking. I'll admit, the backyard is impressive. Being so close to such a busy road, I never would have expected such serenity. With the backyard being the size of half a football field, I'm surprised they built the house so close to the road. But, back in the early eighteen hundreds, they didn't have four lane roads. So, there was probably a decent sized front yard too. I wonder how the view from that little four pane window out front was back then.

"Emma! Look! In there!" Jake takes off towards the bottom of the barn and I run after him.

Standing in the doorway, we can see a dark cat hiding under some wood scraps. Of course, Jake tries to pet it, but the cat just hisses and runs in further. Jake knows no boundaries when it comes to animals. It's a wonder that he hasn't been severally hurt by one yet.

"Stay out of there you two! You don't know what could be in there!" I turn and Gram is sitting up on the back porch stairs. My eyes dart down to her hand, checking for a forbidden cigarette but they are both gripping a coffee cup. Sometimes, she can be irritating but right now, I'm thankful that she is here. She's the only one Jake seems to listen to.

"You see that cat, Grammy?" Jake runs up the stairs so fast that he trips and for a second, I fear he's going to tumble back down. Thankfully my arms stretch out just far enough to push him forward.

"No, but by the sounds of it, the poor thing wants to be left alone. You have this whole yard to play in, stay out of the barn." Gram warns.

"We will." I assure her. That's no place I want to go anyways. From the dirt floors to the leaning piles of wood, it looks like the perfect scene for a horror movie. Fits right in with the rest of this place.

"Stay away from that brook too! You only need a teaspoon of water to drown. I'm not sure how deep that is but we don't need find out from anyone drowning." Gram is a very paranoid individual and that's probably where I get it from. Dad and Grandpa are always telling me I sound like my grandmother.

"Go swimming?" Jake's head tilts when he asks, and I swear smokes going to start pouring out of her ears. But it doesn't. Gram has more patience than anyone I have ever met. I guess being the oldest of seven kids and having to help raise your younger siblings, plus four kids of your own and, all of their friends, would make caring for your grandkids a breeze.

"No, Jake. We only swim in pools. And remember, there must be an adult watching." I remind him. Sometimes Dad brings us to the beach with his friends, but I don't think Jake remembers and I'm not about to mention it. That's something that he wouldn't forget or stop nagging about. We still have a few months before it's warm enough to go swimming anyways.

"Emma's right, Jake." Gram holds up a finger as she bursts into a coughing fit. "So, if you want to continue playing outside, you need to listen to your sister."

"I will." And just like that, Jake is onto the next adventure. Luckily for me, he hears Blue's Clues when he opens the back door and heads inside. I don't know how Gram used to babysit so many kids at once. I can hardly keep up with Jake most days.

"Grammy..." I begin as I sit next to her on the step. "Marie says that this place is haunted." Her arms wrap around me, and the comforting scent of her cucumber melon body spray soothes my nerves a little.

"Lower your voice." She whispers into my hair. "Your Uncle Alan had some experiences years ago when we lived here. Unfortunately, this is the only place I could find for us to live on such a short notice. It's also the cheapest. Once we find somewhere else, we will be moving. This is not a place I plan on staying longer than we have to. It will work for now though." Pausing to take a breath, her arm tightens around me. "This won't be the first house we have shared with the other side."

My throat tightens. Were Marie's stories true? My grandfather has always been a farmer, so they have always lived in old farmhouses. Grandpa frequently talks about the white house on a hill in Unity. One time he was home alone sitting in his favorite rocking chair, which was probably a rare moment since they had four kids, he kept getting poked hard in his ribs. Finally, when he had enough and told whatever it was to *knock it off*, it did. Until the next time anyways. Aunt Karen had also found a lot of Jehovah Witness books in the top of the barn. Not long after, Grams wooden cross that hangs by a hook, was found upside down. They moved out shortly after that.

"Would you like corn chowder for supper?" Gram's corn chowder is the best. Not that I've had any to compare it to, but everyone loves hers. It's the ultimate comfort food, just what I need right about now. "I'll peel the potatoes if you want to put everything we need on the table."

"Okay." She smiles and I follow her inside. Helping Gram cook has always been my favorite thing to do. That is as long as I don't have to peel potatoes. Gram makes it look so easy with her favorite wooden handles knife, but it's really not. I'd rather open ten cans with this old church key can opener.

In the kitchen, Gram's eyes keep wandering to the dumbwaiter next to the table.

"What's in there? Can we open it?" After the question leaves my lips, I'm not sure I really want to see inside. What if it leads directly up to the room above us with the little window?

"Yeah, sure, go ahead. There's just some shelves." Grandpa chimes in and opens the dumbwaiter door. "You could even climb in there is you wanted too."

I'm not usually adventurous but since Gram and Grandpa are right here, what could happen? Grandpa moves a chair so that I can climb in.

I peek my head in and all I see are shelves on both sides and a door on the opposite side leading into Gram and Grandpa's bedroom. Seems harmless enough.

"It is spacious in here! This could actually make for the perfect hiding spot." Six of the shelves are empty. As Grandpa shines a flashlight up on the top shelf, which happens to wrap all the way around since it's above the doors, I notice that there is an absurd amount of black pepper packets. Grabbing a handful, I squat down and hold it out for them to see. "There has to be thousands of pepper packets up there..." Before I can finish Gram cuts me off.

"Put those back and get out of there!" Something in her tone frightens me. Quickly, I do as she says. I have only heard that tone a couple times and it's not something you question.

Once the door is closed, I decide to push my luck a little. "Why would those be in there? And just scattered around? Why didn't they keep then in a box or something?" I ask but Gram's back to peeling potatoes. I turn to Grandpa, but he start whistling as he walks into the living room. Somethings up. Gram always says that she knows when something is wrong because Grandpa whistles.

"Someone put them there for a reason." The knife in her hand stills as she glares at me over her glasses. "So, unless you want to find out that reason, I suggest you leave them alone."

I have no problem leaving them alone, I'm curious as to why they are there. Who wouldn't be? "Is it a superstition?" Gram is always warning us about breaking mirrors, not walking under ladders or how you should throw spilled salt over your shoulder. Along with many others.

"Just leave the pepper alone." Her hazel eyes peer over her glasses again and I know better than to push the subject any further, for now anyways.

Chapter Three

After too much corn chowder, I head to my room. Just like every time I pass that wooden cross, I glance at it and hope that it's not upside down. It's not, thank goodness. Honestly, I'm not sure what I would do if it was. I'm not even sure if I would be surprised. Hopefully I never have to find out.

To get to my room, I have to go through my grandparents' room. Gram has two cockatiels in the corner of their room. They are always so loud, but not tonight. They are oddly quiet for not being covered up. Stopping in front of the white wired cage, one of the little birds is laying on the bottom of the cage with its black eyes wide open. Staring at me. Before I can stop myself, a blood curdling scream escapes my lungs.

"Emma! What happened?" Dad and Grandpa run into the room, and I can hear Gram wheezing behind them.

"Is everything alright?" Gram asks breathlessly.

I can't seem to form the words, so I point towards the cage, stumbling over Baby, Grams fourteen-year-old little black and white dog. Baby doesn't move. Instead, she stands there, bearing what's left of her teeth and growls into the closet under the stairs.

"Emma, go into the living room with your grandmother." I hear dad's voice, but everything is black, and I can't seem to move. "Emma." Finally, my vision comes back, and I follow Gram and her green oxygen hose. Not that it does much good, because I can still hear them talking.

"Dad, this bird is stiffer than a two by four. Are you sure it was alive when you fed them this morning?"

"Of course, I'm sure, Jacob. Don't you think I would have noticed it laying there when I changed out the newspaper?"

"How long do you think this one will live, now that it's girlfriend's dead?"

"Probably a few days. I hope your mother doesn't bring home anymore pets."

Dad starts laughing. "You know she will."

Grandpa chuckles but puts on a straight face when he walks past Gram and I with the rolled-up newspaper.

What do you do with a dead bird? People get buried, sometimes cremated and stuffed into a necklace or vase. Dogs and cats get buried, sometimes cremated and stuffed into a necklace or vase as well. Fish get flushed. But what about birds? Obviously, you can't flush a bird. Could a bird be cremated? Would Gram want the keep its ashes?

"You guys could show a little sympathy, you know." Gram says with her hands on her hips. "And I will bring home as many animals as I wish." As far back as I can remember, Gram has always taken in some animal if one of her friends no longer wants it. Must be where Dad and I learned it from.

Grandpa laughs and shakes his head. He knows she's right. Gram is always right.

"You're going to bury that, right?" Gram states rather than questions. Guess I wasn't the only one wondering this.

"Well what else am I going to do with it, Rose?" Grandpa huffs. "Go get a shovel, Jacob."

The kitchen door shuts and Gram mumbles something as she scrunches her face and sticks her tongue out. This is a face she makes often, and it always makes us laugh. Except for right now, when I can still see the little black eyes staring at me when I close my eyes.

I can't bring myself to walk back through my grandparent's bedroom. Luckily for me I can also go through Dad and Jake's bedroom to get to mine. With a layout like this, I wonder what these rooms were used for back when it was built. Gram said she thinks that it used to be an Inn of some sort. There's only one bathroom but since this place was built thirty years prior to indoor plumbing it very well could have been.

The closer I get to Dad's room, the clearer I hear Jake. "Yeah, I like playing outside. Vroom vroom. You like fast cars? My daddy tells me about *all* of his old fast cars. You can ask him."

Who's he talking to? To my surprise, when I walk into the oversized bedroom, Jake is sitting alone playing with his Hot

Wheels. "Jake who were you talking to?" I look around, not sure what I expect to see.

"My friend." He shrugs his shoulders and goes back to pushing his little cars around the orange plastic tracks.

I look around one more time but it's still just the two of us. *I guess he is around that age for imaginary friends.* I try to comfort myself as I walk into my room. Immediately I spot Tiggy, my orange cat, curled up in a ball on my bed. He's been going wild these last few days. Him and Baby love chasing each other through the circle of rooms. It's actually quite entertaining. Especially when they hit the linoleum in the living room and slide across the room into the T.V stand.

Wait.

Didn't Marie say that her brother had an imaginary friend that lived in his truck? "Jake!" I barge into dad's room, but he isn't there. Panic takes over and I run out into the living room. "Gram, where's Jake?" Frantically pulling the curtains open, I scan the driveway and busy road. Jake's nowhere in sight. My heart stops. As annoying as he can be, he is still my little brother. It's up to me to keep him safe.

Gram sits up quickly, prompting another coughing fit. "He's in the shower. Is everything alright?" The volume of the TV quiets and Baby jumps off the couch.

"Um... Yeah, I guess so." *Breathe.* I repeat to myself all the way back to my room. Grandpa has said that Uncle Alan often exaggerates stories. I can only hope this is one of his over-the-top stories.

Chapter Four

"Where's that light coming from? Did someone leave a light on up here before they closed it off?" Something feels heavy, pulling at my feet, as I follow the long hallway towards the well-lit doorway. Attempting to shake my feet, in hopes to set them free doesn't do anything. Glancing down, there are bulky chains tangled around my ankles.

"What in the world?" Tugging at the chains just causes them to clang louder.

A massive black shadow catches my attention. My eyes travel back to the doorway. Leaning forward just a little gives me a clear view inside the spacious room with purple walls. Sitting in the middle of the room, directly under the ceiling light, there is a tall man dressed in black, perched on a stool. Calmness washes over me as I take a deep breath.

"Who are you?" I feel like I should be frightened but I'm not.

The man's head gradually lifts. The hood of his jacket conceals his eyes but he's grinning, exposing his decaying sharp teeth.

I gasp and tumble backwards.

His head continues to lift, and his eyes are monstrous. My throat closes and I'm frozen. As his mouth opens, I want to look away, but I can't. Abruptly, he screams a horrific shriek and the light bulb above him shatters. Darkness takes over.

"Help! HELP ME!"

"Emma! Wake up!" As my eyes jolt open, Gram's arms are wrapped around me and she's kissing the top of my head. "Grammy's right here. Everything's okay."

Tears stream down my cheeks and I start hyperventilating.

"Shh..." Gram's grips loosens, and I finally manage to take a deep breath.

"There... there's a light on upstairs." I blurt out.

"I'll have your grandfather check it out. Would you like to come out into the living room with me and watch TV?" Her voice is calm but her arms quiver around me and I can hear her trying to control her breathing.

I nod and grab my fuzzy blanket. In the dim light, I can see her green oxygen cord coming through my Grandparents' room. Even though I don't want to walk past the bird cage, I grip Gram's arm, close my eyes and follow her.

● ● ●

Visions of that man are burned into my eyelids, and I quickly open my eyes. The light streaming from the kitchen reminds me of the purple room.

I'm awake now. Gram won't let anything happen to me.

The coffee aroma comforts me, as I know that means Grandpa is awake too. Nothing scary can happen during the day, right? It's like once the coffee has been started, everything spooky and evil crawl back into hiding.

"Everything alright Emmy?" Grandpa's sitting at the kitchen table working on his word search book. I take the seat in the wooden chair beside him, he puts his pen in his book and pushes it aside. Letting me know that I have his full attention. Only I don't know what to say.

"Charles, can you check to see if there are any lights on upstairs? That could be a fire hazard, you know." Gram sits in the chair next to me and sips on her coffee. Guilt floods me as I listen to her wheezing and watch her hands tremble, almost causing her coffee to splash out of her porcelain cup.

Grandpa's brows furrow as he looks from Gram to me. "A light on? Now why would you think there is a light on?"

"I saw it, Grandpa." The nightmare replays in my mind once again and I shudder.

"You did?" Attempting to disguise his grin, he coughs into his handkerchief. Grandpa has never been one to quickly assume there could be ghosts. He will exhaust every other possibility before admitting that's what it could be.

"Charles." Gram glares at him and he takes one last sip of his coffee before standing up.

"Alright, fine. I'll go outside and see if I see any lights on." I don't care that he's only going out to check to humor Gram, at least I don't have to check it out myself.

Nearly ten minutes later, Grandpa marches through the door. Bringing with him a faint smell of cigar smoke. "Well, I'll be dammed." It *is* on. "I'll have to see if Jacob can borrow a ladder from Troy. Maybe I can climb through Alan's old bedroom window to shut it off."

"What do you need a ladder for, Dad?" Dad emerges from the living room rubbing his eyes. "What time is it anyways?"

"Someone left a light on upstairs. When you see your brother today at work, want to ask him if we can borrow one?"

"Yeah. It's only 4:30?" After grabbing a Pepsi out of the fridge, Dad slips on his jacket and heads outside.

Just as I finish my homework, I hear the rumble of Dad's truck pulling into the driveway, letting us know he's home from work. My heart thuds against my chest as I follow Grandpa outside. Dad's already leaning the extended ladder against the front porch roof.

Grandpa stops at the bottom of the ladder. "You want to go first, Emma?" *Nope*.

"Oh, I'm not going up there." No way would I ever go up there.

"There's nothing up there that's going to hurt you." Grandpa chuckles and starts up the ladder.

"You don't know that." Neither do I, nor do I care to find out. I watch closely as he climbs through the window, half expecting the guy from my dream, no, nightmare, to attack him.

It worries me that the window was so easy to open. Or at least that's how Grandpa made it seem. Shouldn't it have been locked? Possibly even painted shut?

A few long minutes pass before Grandpa climbs out of the window. "It looks like someone has done some painting since Alan lived here. It's actually pretty nice up there. I'm surprised they closed it off and didn't make an apartment."

"What color is the room that had the light on?" I'm not sure if I actually want to know. *Please tell me white*.

"It's a darker color." As he shrugs his shoulders, I remember that Grandpa is color blind. "Back when Alan lived here, they were all white." *So, it's not white anymore.*

"Was there anything in the rooms?" A cold chill runs over me. *Please say no*.

"Just a stool. And it's a good thing, otherwise I wouldn't have been able to reach the chain to shut the light off."

No. No. No. My heart is pounding so loud that I can hear it in my ears. Why did I have to ask? Surely, I would have been better off not knowing.

We just moved here, and I already hate this house. Why couldn't we have moved somewhere else? Maybe somewhere with a little less *history*.

Chapter Five

Sleep hasn't come easy for me these last few months. I've never felt this exhausted. My assignments from school have begun to pile up again. My focus on staying awake during class overshadows my ability to stay focused on the teacher and lesson. Up until this year, I have always made Honor Roll. Dad, Gram and Grandpa haven't come out and said it, but I can feel their disappointment. Neither of my grandparents graduated high school or even made it past the fifth grade. Two out of four of their kids reached a graduating level. Back then that was accepted, expected in most circumstances. Especially if you grew up on farms like they did. We don't live on a farm, so my lack of academic success will not be expected and certainly not accepted.

My time after school is spent keeping a closer than usual eye on Jake and his little red Camaro. He brings it everywhere and treats it just like a friend. The other day, Jake was playing outside while Grandpa mowed the lawn, and he just took off. We found him splashing in the brook, little red car in hand. I've never seen Gram so flustered. That was the second time I had to call 911 for Gram and the first time I had to find and pick up ninety-six itty bitty nitroglycerin tablets of the floor before Baby ate them. Gram's home now. Turns out it was a panic attack. With her health issues I know she lives in fear of having another stroke or heart attack. *I* live in fear of her having another stroke or heart attack. So, we can't take situations like that lightly.

The loud footsteps above my room start every night around 9:30. I've tried covering my ears with my hands, earmuffs, and a pillow but it still doesn't block it out. Music helped but I haven't been able to find my headphones. I was convinced Jake snagged them, but I would have seen him playing with them by now.

Even when I manage to sleep, the same nightmare continues to replay over and over. I can only hope that eventually my body will be so exhausted that I will sleep dreamlessly.

Gram's other bird passed away a week ago and Baby stands in front of the closet space under the stairs and growls for most of the night, every night. That is until Grandpa has had enough and tells her to go lay down. She doesn't listen though, a few minutes later she's back to growling. She may only weigh eight and a half pounds but that doesn't stop her from thinking she can protect us.

On my way to the kitchen, I notice someone has slid a shelf in front of that closet entrance. It feels a little less chilling, but something still feels eerie. Almost as if something is hiding in there, watching as I walk by. Waiting for its chance. I run the last few feet, stopping in the kitchen doorway.

"Must be nice to sleep all day." Dad jokes and takes a bite of his bologna sandwich.

"It's only ten, Dad." If I could sleep at night, I wouldn't have to sleep during the day. I've always been the first to fall asleep. Sleeping past seven in the morning never happened for me. Now, I finally fall asleep around four, when I hear Grandpa get up because that's the only time I feel safe. Too bad Grandpa can't keep me safe from the nightmares as well.

"If you weren't practicing routines for cheerleading all night, you'd probably sleep better. At the rate I hear you stomping around, you're going to wear the paint off the floor." Gram chimes in as she cleans the table, tossing Dad's excess salt from his sandwich over her shoulder.

"How many times do I have to tell you guys that I am not the one making the noise? You all know that I have never been one to stay up all night."

"Jacob, are you still letting Jake eat candy and watch TV with you at bedtime?"

"Of course not, Mom. Jake falls asleep before me, and he stays asleep all night. It's probably just an animal that somehow got upstairs. Remember that time you dug a critter out of the wall in the apartment on Tremont Street? That little thing created all kinds of ruckus. We were surprised to find that it was just a kitten."

I remember that tiny black kitten. It was so terrified. Gram prayed that since we saved it, maybe it wouldn't bring her bad luck every time it crossed her path. That's one of Gram's superstitions that I don't believe. Pippy was a great cat and still to this day, I have no idea what happened him.

"Well, were about to find out." I turn towards Grandpa and he's carrying a hammer and a bucket. What's he up to?

"Charles, just what do you think you're going to do?" Gram jumps to her feet and follows him to the hall between the living room and Dad's room.

Whatever is happening, I know by the sheer look of panic on Gram's face, it's not going to end well. Grabbing the phone, I run after them.

Facing the faux wall, Grandpa continues, "I just went to see Karen. Some things have happened, and they are going to stay with us for a while." As he raises the hammer Gram shrieks. My thumb hovers over the call button.

"You can't just tear down a wall! We are only renting this space down here, and just for a short time, I may add!" Her hands are trembling and her voice cracks like she's about to start crying.

"Sure, we can. Jacob and Troy can replace it when we move out. Rose, this house is going to be overcrowded with extra people here. There's nothing wrong with the upstairs."

"Have you lost your ever-loving mind? You're going to go to hell for unleashing what's up there! It's sealed off for a reason!" I completely agree. I'm not religious nearly as much as Gram, but I know what I felt, and I don't wish for my nightmares to become my reality. It was definitely sealed to keep that part separate. Why? I don't know or care enough to want to find out.

"You worry too much. The only thing up there is a squirrel or chipmunk. Tiggy will take care of that." Grandpa argues.

There's no way something that small could be making so much noise. And at the same time every night? I don't think so. Tiggy may be able to catch a few mice but whatever Baby keeps growling at, he wants no part of. I get the feeling that whatever is up there is far worse.

"Jacob, tell your father this is not a good idea!" All eyes are on Dad and I'm hoping he will take Gram's side, but he just shakes his head.

"Sorry Mom, I agree with Dad. I'm sure they only built this wall so that they didn't have to heat it. Could you imagine how much that would cost?" Of course, this would be Dad's concern.

"I'm not letting my grandkids sleep up there! If you two want to open it then *you two* are going to be the ones moving up there!"

"They'll be fine. A little ghost isn't going to hurt anyone. If it was, don't you think it would have done so by now?" Grandpa taunts.

Gram's face pales. "Do you not remember what happened to Alan back when he lived here?" Tears are on the verge of streaming down her face. "Emma, grab me a chair." Running into the kitchen, I grab one of the wooden chairs but as I turn around, through the window, I see Jake standing on the back porch railing. Dammit! This is what happens if no one is watching him for just two minutes.

I drop the chair and try not to let the back door slam against Gram's china cabinet. "Jake, what are you doing up here?" I ask, keeping my voice low so that I don't startle him.

Ignoring me, he continues pushing his little red car up the post. "Vroom Vroom!"

Slowly, I step closer to him and pull him down. "Jake, you can't be up there! You could have fallen. Do you see how high up this is?" It's easily a twelve-foot drop, and Jake has never been able to balance very well.

"My car wanted to climb the tower." He slumps and starts crying.

Why has no one taken this car from him yet? Every time he's caught doing something he knows he shouldn't be he blames that damn car. "Well, this is not safe. Let's go find something else to do." Thankfully, Jake wipes his nose on his sleeve and leads the way back inside.

Someone must have grabbed the chair for Gram since she's now sitting in it. "Fine! You do what you want but don't say I didn't warn you two! Wait until I get back to the living room though. If some ghost flies down the stairs, I'm not going to be the first one to be possessed." After a few steps, she stops and turns around to face Dad and Grandpa but doesn't say anything.

With that being said, Grandpa starts swinging the hammer and the drywall crumbles at his feet. Once the dust settles, we can see the old well-used wooden stairs. Next to a hole in the wall, revealing the wood lath that was once covered in plaster, are two buttons, one above the other.

"What are the buttons for, Dad?" I ask from the security of the living room doorway. I'm not sure why the living room feels safe, nothing about this house gives off a safe vibe. Gram is in here though, that's as much reassurance I'm going to get.

"It's a push button light switch. There should be one at the top of the stairs too." Dad says as he and Grandpa step over the pile of crumbled drywall. Jake bolts past them and instinctively, I chase after him.

Wait a second.

The air feels heavier. The walls surrounding me are no longer white. They are more yellow, as if people smoked up here a lot. The linoleum that was under my feet minutes ago has been replaced with chipped gray painted wood floors. *Shit*.

I'm upstairs.

"Dammit Jake." I mumble.

I guess it couldn't hurt to take a look around. Besides, I'm already up here. Dad and Grandpa will keep us safe. Right?

It's spacious up here. It's astonishing that they didn't turn it into an apartment. I haven't seen any outlets or heat registers but according to Dad, that would be nothing to put in compared to the potential revenue.

The room at the top of the stairs to the left is the one above my room. To my surprise, the walls are purple. *The same exact purple as the room in my nightmares.* How is this even possible? A shiver runs through my body, forcing me to step back.

"I thought you shut that light off, Dad?" Dad asks Grandpa as he walks past me and reaches up for the chain, pushing the stool out of his way. With the snap of the chain the light shuts off.

"I did. There must be a short somewhere."

A short alright.

Or ghosts.

"Take the bulb out!" Gram yells from the bottom of the stairs. "We don't need the house burning down! Maybe when your done stirring up the spirits upstairs, you can play with the ones in the basement while you shut the damn breakers off!"

Dad continues looking around the purple room, probably measuring up the work that would need to be done. He does this everywhere we go. With being a drywaller for about sixteen years, I assume it's just habit.

Across the hall there is a much smaller room. So small there isn't even a window. With the door open, I can see the walls are pink, like Pepto pink. After my eyes finally adjust, I notice a large dark spot on the wall. Did someone paint over something? What were they trying to cover up? Unintentionally, I take a few steps towards it. As my fingertips trace over the dark pink area, the walls begin to feel like they are closing in, trapping me. My heart races and cautiously, I step back, unable to remove my eyes from that spot. The door creaks behind me and I run out before it slams behind me.

What. The. Hell. Was. That.

Back in the hallway, Jake darts past me to the other end. Nearly knocking me over. I'm glad there is a railing separating the hallway and the drop to the stairwell. Otherwise, he would have ran off the edge. His eye surgery as a toddler may have corrected his eyes but he has no concept of heights or his surroundings.

Next to the pink room there is another long narrow hallway. At the very end there's a door. The longer I stare at it, the faster my heart pounds and I can feel the hair on the back of my neck stand.

I don't think I want to see anymore of the rooms this house has to offer. With each one, something inside of me feels darker. I'm lost on how to describe it. It's bright enough up here but it just feels dark. This is probably why they haven't turned it into an apartment.

"That's your Uncle Alan's old train room." I jump when something touches my shoulder and I realize it's just Grandpa's hand.

"Emma! Come see!" Jake's squeaky voice echoes down both hallways. Dad starts down the hall towards Jake and we follow.

To the left, there is an excessively large room with an apple red floor. Covering the floor is a thick layer of dust. In the dust, there are footprints and other random marks. I can tell some are from Jake's little bare feet. Under the window, there is a set that leads over to the other door in the room and out into the narrow hallway. I'm not sure what the other prints and markings could be from. I know if I ask, Dad and Grandpa are just going to put the blame on a mouse or some other rodent. Which I know that's not what they are from. They are a considerable size. Some being a little bigger than Jake's prints and others bigger than Dad's feet. These are not just footprints though. Where the prints are in the dust, there's also scratches in the red paint on the floor.

What happened in here?
● ● ●

"That's an interesting color for a floor, isn't it? Your grandfather was right, someone has painted since Alan lived here. This used to be gray, not red." Gray feels more fitting. Even if this whole place was painted white, it would do nothing to mask the darkness.

"I told you. Little Alan's room was in the room across the hall." Faintly I hear Grandpa start whistling.

I squeeze Dad's arm and follow him into the next room. I'm not sure if I can handle anymore dark feelings.

The white walls and gray floor are the same as the bedroom's downstairs. Only these walls haven't been recently painted. The paint on the ceiling is starting to flake off. The oval sticker in the window is clearer than when Jake pointed it out shortly after we moved in. It says Tot Finder above a firefighter holding a small child. I guess I can see how he thought it was an actual person.

As I step through the doorway, any ill feelings have been replaced with calmness. The air is much lighter in here. For the first time since we have moved in, I'm able to take a deep breath. I can't remember the last time my heart was beating at a slow steady pace like it is now. This is really strange. What is it about this room? Why is it so different than the rest of the rooms up here? Why is it different than the rest of the rooms in this house?

I really like this room.

I try to envision how I would set it up and turn it into my own space. My bed could go under the window since the ceiling isn't peeling that bad in that area. My dresser would go perfect on this wall with the slanted ceiling. Gram wouldn't be on board, but I bet Dad and Grandpa would let me paint. Even if they say no, I have plenty of posters to cover the yellow stained walls.

I can't believe I'm even considering this.

There's no way Gram will let me have this room.

Would I actually want to be up here? Would it always feel this peaceful? None of the other rooms feel this way. What's so different about this room?

I skim the room again. "Can this be my room?" I blurt before I can give it another thought.

Grandpa's whistling gets louder. Maybe this *is* a terrible idea. I wait for one of them to answer me. When they don't I turn to make sure they are still in here. Grandpa's eyes are fixated on the far corner while he continues whistling.

"Sure, if you want it to be." Dad says hesitantly. "But we're going to have to take care of this chipped paint first."

After one more glance around the room, I'm certain that I want this to be my room.

Chapter Six

At last, it's Friday and my best friend Olivia is helping me move into my new bedroom upstairs. The last two days have been pretty quiet and uneventful. Maybe I was just letting paranoia get the best of me. Maybe this house isn't so bad after all.

"I wish I could live here with the ghosts. Remember that time something scratched the bottoms of my feet when I was sleeping at my house? Sometimes I hear my name being called from my closet but that's the most that happens there anymore."

"Oh, I remember all too clearly." It's been almost two years since, and I still can't bring myself to tell her what I really saw that night, or any other time I have been there. I get chills just thinking about it.

Olivia goes on as we head upstairs for the fourth time. "What's in that room at the end of the hall?"

Ah yes, *that* room. The one that I have yet to see. I'm sure it looks just like these rooms, but I just can't bring myself to open the door. I try not to even look down the hall as I run past it. It just has a creepy vibe. "That's Uncle Alan's old train room."

A grin spreads across her face, I know that look all too well. "Let's go check it out!"

"Or we could not." I suggest in hopes that she agrees.

"What, are you to chicken?" Olivia's now clucking and flapping like a chicken. It's hard to have a serious conversation with her when she does things like this. It's a great distraction though.

"Yes." I'm not afraid to admit it. Especially when the footsteps have stopped and the goosebumps on my arms have finally gone away. I'm not going to jinx that.

"Can I go check it out then? I'll wait for you to go downstairs."

"What are you guys checking out?" I jump when I hear Aunt Karen directly behind me.

"Ah! Why does everyone find joy in scaring me?" My frustration grows as Olivia and Aunt Karen laugh.

"Because it's too easy." Olivia blurts and I roll my eyes.

"Olivia wants to go see the train room."

Aunt Karen shakes her head adamantly, "You girls are on your own there."

"No, Olivia is on her own." I correct.

"Oh, come on Olivia. I'll go with you." David, Aunt Karen's boyfriend shouts from the hall. Somehow that doesn't startle me but then again, I could hear his footsteps coming up the stairs. David is a loud guy and in times like this, I'm completely okay with it.

Aunt Karen and I trail behind them, carefully keeping our distance.

"I still can't believe you are okay with living up here. You do know that it's going to get dark up here, right?" She stops halfway down the narrow hallway. "You can go ahead, I'm good where I am."

Taking a few steps closer, I watch Olivia and David take a step down into the room. Why does this room have that step? None of the other rooms have that. Unlike the size of the other rooms in this house, this one is smaller. Not quite as small as the pink room but smaller than my room. The flowered wallpaper is stained yellow and peeling. Straight ahead there's a poster of a teddy bear holding some colorful balloons. I was wrong. This room has no comparison to the others.

"Emma, this room is cool! You should make this your room instead. We will have to replace the window since it doesn't open. But that's not a big deal. I'm sure it would get hot in the summer."

"If you like it so much David, you can have it as your room." The hairs on the back of my neck stand up and the tightness in my throat is back. Suddenly, I feel the urge to run but my feet won't move. Just like in my nightmare. *Breathe*. I repeat until everything goes black.

"You'd be sleeping in there without me." I hear Aunt Karen mumble. "Show me your room."

Someone grabs my arm and begins pulling me away from this strange room. My vision starts to come back the further we get. "What was that? I think I should see a doctor."

Aunt Karen glares at me, "*That's* why I won't get too close to that room." I wait for her to elaborate but she doesn't. "Which ones have you seen?"

"Excuse me?" Which what?

"*Them*." Lifting her head towards the doorway, my eyes follow, and I blink a few times to make sure the old lady in the wheelchair is indeed there and not just in my imagination. Everything about her looks sad. From her dark eyes to her long gray hair but most of all, her sunken posture. "She won't hurt you." Aunt Karen whispers.

That does nothing to alleviate the pressure building in my head or the sudden lack of air around me. Gram always says Karen and I are a lot like herself. All three of us have always been able to see more than most. This doesn't bring me comfort though. I would be perfectly content if I didn't see *more*.

"I have this reoccurring nightmare. It started shortly after we moved in. It felt more like déjà vu. There was a man dressed in black…"

"Like a grim reaper but with sharp teeth?"

"Like something out of a horror film." I nod and cringe at the memory that's now imbedded into my brain. I've never been a fan of scary movies, even less so now.

"That's the thing that used to lift your Uncle Alan off the floor and hold him against the wall. It's possessive. I will never forget the first time I saw it take over Alan. I came up here to see what he was doing and when he turned around, his eyes were black, and he just kept chanting. Whatever he was saying wasn't in English."

"You saw all of this and are still moving in? That doesn't make any sense to me."

"It's only temporary and I know the *others* won't let anything happen to any of us."

Temporary. I chuckle. That's the word Gram used too. And yet, were still here with no talk of moving anymore. I let what she just said replay in my head again. I guess so far no one has been physically hurt. Maybe she's right.

"Just keep your distance from that room."

There's no way I will be going near there. "You don't have to tell me twice."

"Emma, you want some headphones?" David's voice carries down the hall.

Headphones? That's random. Although, I still haven't bought a new pair so it's kind of convenient.

The lady in the wheelchair leisurely moves into the red room across the hall before she disappears. This intrigues me because according to almost all scary movies, ghost only appear at nighttime. Why am I seeing one now? *I must be hallucinating.*

I rub my eyes, probably a little too hard since I'm now seeing spots and my black headphones, that have been missing for months, dangling from David's hand. Where did he find them?

"They look practically brand new. If you don't want them, I'll give them to…"

"Where did you find those?" I ask, cutting him off.

"On the floor in that room." *That's not possible.*

"You guys are messing with me." They are the only two that I know of to go in there. Glancing between them, I wait for one of their expressions to give something away, but they look just as confused as I feel. Maybe someone came up here while I was at school? There's no way Gram would come up here, even if she could. Dad goes to work before I go to school, and I get home before him. I would have seen Jake come up here. That leaves Grandpa, I'll have to ask him.

"No, seriously Emma. They were there when we opened the door." Olivia adds.

"These are mine." My hand starts shaking as I reach for them. "I haven't seen them in a few months or so."

"Must be the ghost." David and Olivia utter at the same time before laughing.

"I wouldn't be laughing if I were you two." Aunt Karen scolds, sounding remarkably like Gram. "We're going to pick up something for dinner. Any suggestions?"

Way to change the subject Aunt Karen, or maybe this is her way of ending it. "Whatever you guys want to make is fine."

Anything they make is usually good and different than the ten different dinners Gram and I usually rotate through.

David sighs. "You're the pickiest eater I know, that's why we're asking you."

"I'll be fine. If I don't like it, I'll eat something else."

He shakes his head, clearly unimpressed with my answer. "Alright, we'll be back in a bit."

As they start down the stairs, I close my bedroom door. How does that saying go? *Out of sight out of mind?* That can work for anything, right? Ghost included?

"So, what should we do tonight? We could sleep in that scary room."

I laugh but Olivia just stares at me. "Oh. You're serious?"

"Come on! Just for one night? I was just in there and there's nothing in there Emma. Well, besides your headphones." Olivia shrugs and sits beside me on my bed. "What else is there to do?"

"Ensley will be here soon, maybe we could go for a walk or something."

"I bet Ensley would sleep in there."

"You can ask her." I'm not entirely sure Ensley would. Sure, we've messed around with some ouija boards but that's different. That was just for fun and nothing scary ever happened.

"Ask me what?" Ensley drops her bag on my bed before sitting down next to it.

Olivia jumps off my bed. "I think that we should sleep in the creepy room tonight! Do you want to?"

"Uh… what's the creepy room? Emma, what do you think?" I think Olivia is too ecstatic to notice Ensley subtly shaking her head at me.

Before I can answer, Olivia adds, "It's down that long hallway at the top of the stairs. Supposably it's haunted."

"There's no way I will go in there, never mind sleep. But if you guys want to, go right ahead." I think I'd sleep in the basement before I'd sleep in that room.

"I'm all set too. I don't need to sleep in there to know the obvious. Clearly the other side lives here too." This is why Ensley and I are such good friends, she is also *gifted*. It's comforting to know that I'm not the only one our age that senses spirits.

"Sorry Olivia. Looks like you're on your own."

"Emma, how is it that this room has a different feel than the entire rest of the house?"

I've been waiting for someone else to notice this. "I haven't figured that out yet." I still don't understand. This room, *my room*, feels as though it's in a completely different house.

"Maybe the other rooms just need some fresh paint!" Olivia and Ensley suggest.

"That's actually not a bad idea!" I highly doubt paint will change anything about the creepy room though. We can just skip that room, maybe even put a lock on it. Would a lock do anything though? "I'll ask my dad and David if we have any paint or if they can buy some."

"Yes! I love painting!" Good, maybe this will keep Olivia's mind occupied.

Unfortunately, we didn't have any paint. But then again, I'm not sure why I would have thought that we would have paint laying around. I can't recall the last time we painted anything. Well, besides Gram spray painting her metal stool that's been passed down and painted every color of the rainbow.

"I tried to get a shade close to the pink that's already on the wall. That will make it easier to cover up." David explains while prying open the gallon of Pepto-Bismol pink paint.

"A completely different color would have sufficed." I think I would have preferred white. Sure, it would take more work to cover but I think it would help change the atmosphere.

He sighs. "Emma, you didn't say what color."

"It's fine. This should help clean it up a little."

"Your aunt and I also grabbed some light bulbs. I have no idea if the celling lights work up here but that will help brighten it up too."

I'll admit, the lights definitely help make it feel slightly less *dark*. Although, that dark spot on the wall seems even darker with the light on.

"I wonder what they were trying to cover up here." The dark spot disappears after Ensley rolls the new paint over it.

Almost an hour later, we finally set the rollers and brushes down. Now that the whole room is painted, and all the blemishes are gone, this room has an entirely different feel. "Maybe we could add some couches and make a little sitting room in here."

Ensley glances around the small room and smiles. "Oh! That's a great idea!" I just know her head is swirling with ideas on how to decorate this space.

"So, I think we should paint the creepy room next!"

"Nope!" Ensley exclaims and I agree.

Maybe it's just my subconscious but I'm almost certain that dark spot is returning. "Uh… Ensley?"

"Yeah?"

"I think you may need to go over that spot again."

"What are you talking about?" Paint drips from the roller onto her sneaker and the floor as she stands. "*What?* I don't understand, it was just gone."

Intently, we watch as the roller glides over, once again making the dark spot vanish. In no time it matches the rest of the walls.

No sooner does Ensley set the roller down, the spot darkens all over again.

"What the hell?" The three of us mutter.

"Girls, dinner is done!" Aunt Karen shouts from the bottom of the stairs.

● ● ●

"Maybe the paint just needs to dry?" Olivia suggests.

"Yeah, maybe you're right. Let's check back tomorrow." Something inside me already has a feeling that this spot will be even darker then.

Dinner was just as good as I figured it would be, and I only picked out the chunks of ham from the otherwise good pasta salad.

After lingering in the kitchen for nearly an hour after dinner, I finally muster up the courage to ask, "So, can someone walk us upstairs?"

Grandpa chuckles. "You mean to tell me that the *three* of you girls can't walk upstairs alone?"

"How do you expect to sleep up there?" Aunt Karen jabs David in the ribs, hard enough for him to wince as he grips his side. "Alright, let's go. I'll walk you girls up."

Halfway up the old creaky stairs, he stops. "Alright, good night girls."

"Wait." My eyes glance between him and the creepy room door. "Can you wait until I shut my door?"

"Okay, fine."

Hurrying down the hall, I quickly close my door and ignore David laughing. Everyone seems to find it amusing but I don't see anyone else volunteering to sleep up here.

"Come on guys! I really think we should sleep in the creepy room! Please?" Olivia begs and I shake my head. There is no way she's talking me into this. I want nothing to do with *that* room.

"After what you and Emma have told me? No way."

"Then what are we going to do?" Olivia starts pacing and for a second, I think she's going to grab a blanket and sleep in there by herself.

"Emma, you could see if Sebastian and Asher want to hang out and we could go for a walk." That's not a bad suggestion. Ensley's plugging my hair straightener into the power strip.

Hopefully, Gram doesn't go into Dad's room anytime soon. She would have a fit if she knew there was an extension cord running up through the vent.

"Boring." Olivia rolls her eyes. "What about using a ouija board? We could see if this place is really haunted!"

"Ouch!" Before I look over, I already know Ensley burnt her finger. One of us always is. You'd think by now, we would know to keep our fingers away from the four-hundred-and-fifty-degree metal plates. "Do you just carry one around with you?"

"Even if they actually worked, we don't need one to know this house is haunted." I add quietly.

"Come on, I know you two have done this before. We can make one!" Before we can say no, Olivia is already busy making it. "Emma and Ensley, you have two choices. Either we sleep in that room, or we ask the ghosts a few questions."

Tonight, is not going to be as enjoyable as I had hoped.

Chapter Seven

Well, since I'm not a believer that real ouija boards actually work, I don't see the harm in playing along with this homemade one. It beats sleeping in that room.

Setting the hair straightener down, Ensley turns to face Olivia and I. "I'm not so sure this is a good idea."

"Would you rather go with option A?" Olivia's persistent and always has been. She would make a great lawyer someday.

"How many times have we done this at your house, Ensley?" I ask.

"A few times, I guess."

"And the worst that's happened was the candles blew out. Which very well could have been from the fan in the other room. After all, your mom's bedroom door *was* open." I explain in hopes that she will agree. There's no way I'm sleeping in there and I know Olivia is not dropping this anytime soon.

"But this place is actually haunted though."

"Yeah, I'm fully aware of that." Picking up the opened folder, that now has letters drawn across the top, I hold it out for Ensley to see. "I doubt this is going to work anyways. No offence Olivia."

She shrugs. "None taken."

"You're probably right. Alright, let's do this."

I lower my voice. "How many candles do you think we need?" If Gram knew about my candles or even heard *ouija board* mentioned, she would give us an ear full and probably make us sleep in the living room so that she could keep an eye on us.

"How many do you have?" Ensley asks and I point towards the black metal racks that used to hold my porcelain dolls. Those will be staying in boxes until I can find a new home for them. They're wicked creepy and I'm still too afraid to ask Gram if she was the one who turned them all back around, after I had turned them to face the wall. She says they will be worth money someday. At this point, I could care less about the money.

Olivia chuckles. "That should be more than enough. What about a necklace or something with a string?"

"Let me check." My jewelry box doesn't contain much but there is one thin chained necklace, that I've had since I was really little, hanging on a hook. "Will this work?" The little teddy bear holding a pink stone, spins between us.

"Yep." Ensley and I start lighting the candles as Olivia pulls the chain on the light above us. The room darkens and it starts to feel a little eerie from the flicker of the candles.

I take a deep breath. *Everything will be fine.* Gram, Grandpa, Dad, Jake, Aunt Karen, and David are downstairs. I might feel a little more anxious if it were just us three here. Actually, if it were just the three of us here, there's absolutely no way this would be happening right now.

"Alright Olivia, why don't you start?" I ask as she joins us on the floor.

"What? I'm not the one who has done this before."

"Right but you're the one who is so interested in these ghosts." Ensley points out.

"I think you forgot to write hello." I add, not meaning to be sarcastic.

"What? I didn't realize I was making a Hallmark card."

"Would you just walk into someone's house without saying hello?" Or at least that's why I've heard it's there. After tripping over her overnight bag, Olivia scribbles hello on the folder. "Maybe you should add a smiley face." I can't resist. Ensley and I burst out laughing.

"Come on guys. This won't work if you don't take it serious."

"We're sorry. Please continue."

Olivia hovers the necklace over the makeshift ouija board. "Is there anyone here with us?" In the flicker of the candles the little silver teddy bear starts swaying. It's hard to see but I'm pretty sure Olivia is doing it.

"Ask how many." Ensley whispers. "Hold the necklace over each number and when it starts to move in a circle, that's the answer."

"How many spirits are here?" We lean in and watch closely. Finally, as the necklace is above the three, it starts circling.

"What's your name?" Patiently we wait again as she pauses over each letter. Finally spelling out A B I G A I L.

"Abigail, could you draw us a picture?"

"I don't think ghosts can do that, Olivia." I'm trying to suppress my laugh but if she starts asking for them to make her a sandwich, I can't promise anything.

"You never know. Who else is here? What's your name?" The chain is still as she passes the first three letters. Small circles start to form over G and quickly turn into larger circles.

Ensley and I look at each other and back to Olivia.

"What's the next letter?" Olivia asks and the necklace spins faster until it flies out of her fingertips and across the room, stopping once it ricochets off the wall and falls to the floor.

"Olivia, what the..."

"No." Olivia's mouth moves but it's not her voice. It's closer to a growl. Her blue eyes have now turned black. Is this what happened to Uncle Alan?

My bedroom door whips open, slamming against the wall, blowing the candles out.

Darkness. Complete darkness.

"DAD!"

"JACOB!"

Chapter Eight

My eyes are closed tight, and my palms are pushing against my ears as hard as I can. Even through the rushing sounds of blood running through my body and over the rapid thumping in my chest, I can still hear that growling voice.

"What in hell is going on up here?" Grandpa's voice breaks through, sounding like a whisper.

What if it's not actually Grandpa.

I try to close my eyes tighter, shuddering as the thunderous voice continues to replay in my head. I feel like my heads about to explode.

"Would one of you turn the damn light on?" His stern tone is louder and clearer now.

Something touches my shoulders and an ear-piercing scream echoes off the walls. Even louder than before. I can't be in this house anymore. And of course, I had to choose the room furthest from an exit.

"Emma, stop that screaming! I don't see anything to be afraid of."

I didn't even realize I was screaming again. Warily, I start to open my eyes as someone clicks the light on. Across from me, Ensley is coiled up against my dresser, shaking like I am. Grandpa is standing in the doorway and the hall light is shining behind him. Everything looks a hell of a lot less scary, but it doesn't *feel* any less scary.

"You better not tell your grandmother you're messing around with this crap. I hope you girls got scared good, too. That ought to teach you." He scolds.

"I'm sorry Charles, it was my idea. It won't happen again." Olivia's voice has returned and it's unexpectedly calm. I still can't bring myself to look at her.

"You're right it won't." He closes the door and stomps down the hallway and the stairs. Is it me or are the creaks louder than before?

"What the hell was that?" Ensley blurts.

"I know we weren't taking it serious but was that really necessary?" Still wiry, I gradually turn towards Olivia. Fortunately, her blue eyes have returned and she's now sitting on my bed, looking significantly less frightening.

"What are you guys talking about? What happened? The last thing I remember is your necklace circling over the letter G. After that everything went black."

"*What happened?* You threw Emma's necklace against the wall! And your eyes... they... they were black!"

"And your voice… I don't even know what to compare it to. I've never heard anything like it!"

"That's actually pretty cool! What did I say?" The hint of excitement in Olivia's voice is rather disturbing. I doubt she would find this amusing if she were able to see what happened.

If I wasn't too afraid to sleep up here before, I am now. If I wasn't there would be a good chance that I would ask Olivia and Ensley to leave. I don't want to hear about that damn room. I don't want this crappy ouija board in this house. I don't even want to be in this house. I need to leave.

"All you said was 'no', but it was like wicked creepy!"

"I need to get out of here for a little while." A little while is an understatement. I'm not really sure of where to go but anywhere will be better than spending another minute here.

"I agree with Emma. Let's go Olivia."

I'm incredibly grateful that Grandpa left the hall light on, since the switch is at the other end of the hall. Huddled together anyways, the three of us run down the hall. When Olivia pauses at the top of the stairs, my eyes follow hers.

The single bulb light above us starts swaying, illuminating down the narrow hall in front of us. The creepy room door is wide open, and I wonder if Olivia and Ensley can see what I'm seeing.

A young girl, with ratty brown hair, wearing an old white dress, stands in front of the teddy bear poster, appearing almost translucent. Before I can ask if they see her too, the door slams shut. So hard that the wooden floor beneath our feet quakes.

"SCREW THIS!" I shout as I run down the stairs, avoiding more than half of them.

"I'M OUT!" Darting past me, Ensley jerks the front door at the bottom of the stairs open.

"WAIT FOR ME!" Olivia yells from rather far away. From outside we can see Olivia's just now reaching the bottom of the stairs.

What the hell took her so long?

As my heart pounds, my chest tightens and suddenly it feels like there is a plastic bag over my face. I can't breathe.

The driveway is not far enough.

I start running up the sidewalk. The running doesn't make it easier to breathe but the further I get away from the house, the pressure compressing my ribs lessens. Ahead, there is a well-lit parking lot. My momentum picks up and I don't slow down until I'm standing under the bright light. Seconds later Olivia and Ensley join me, trying to catch their breaths as well.

"I think I'm going to see if my mom can pick me up." Pausing to catch her breath, Olivia continues, "I can't go back there."

"Olivia, can I stay at your house? My mom's probably sleeping."

"You guys are just going to leave me? Olivia, this is your fault! If we had just gone for a walk, none of this would have happened!"

"I'm sorry! I would say you could come too Emma, but I doubt your Gram's going to let you leave this late." As much as I hate to admit it, Olivia's right. Reaching into her pocket, she pulls out her cellphone and presses it to her ear.

Unintentionally, I begin pacing under the bright parking lot light. What am I going to do? My two closest friends are already here, and it's not like I could go with them anyways. Marie lives too far away to go there. I wish Aunt Karen still had her apartment up the street. She would let me stay with her. Just like the time I went to see Hide and Seek with Asher and Stacey. The movie didn't end until almost eleven at night, but I was too afraid to go home. And that was in our old house, which wasn't anywhere near as scary as here.

"Earth to Emma?" Olivia's voice breaks through my thoughts.

"I'm sorry, what did you say?"

"My mom is on her way. We have to meet her at your house. We will get our stuff another time. Maybe you could bring it to school or have your grandpa drop it off at our houses?" They start back towards the house, and I sit on the cool pavement, leaning against the light post.

"Okay. Call me tomorrow?"

"You're not coming with us? What if someone asks where you are?"

"I'm going to stay here for a little while. I don't know. Tell them that we need to move." Surely Gram will want to move now and when Gram makes up her mind, she doesn't stop until she's satisfied.

I'm not sure how long I've been sitting here but it's probably been a few hours since my butt went numb from this hard pavement. The amount of traffic has started to multiply as the sun rises. Slowly I push myself up. Bit by bit I make my way back to the house. Dad's standing at the end of the driveway with a Pepsi in one hand and a cigarette in the other. Even on his days off he's never one to sleep in so this doesn't surprise me. I think I'm too exhausted to be surprised by anything anyways.

"And where have you been all night?" Intently I stare at the orange glow of his cigarette when he takes a drag. "You better go see your grandmother. She's been up all night worrying about you."

"I want to move." My voice comes out quieter than I had anticipated and for a second, I wonder if he even heard me with all the cars that are now passing by.

"Where are we going to move to?" As he exhales, the wind blows the smoke towards me, and I start coughing.

"Anywhere but here would be a good start."

"Even if we wanted to, we wouldn't be able to find a place big enough for all of us now. There's nothing wrong with this house. You need to stop listening to you grandmother and your aunts ghost stories."

"Or maybe you should start taking them more serious. Dad, if you saw what I saw last night, you wouldn't be standing here defending this place!"

With nowhere else to go, I open the kitchen door. Directly on the other side, Gram is sitting at the table with a cup of coffee. Her short gray curly hair is standing up and pointing in all different directions. It's clear that she has been up all night. Shockingly, she doesn't lecture me right away.

"Grammy, can we please move?" I know if I call her Grammy, her mood will soften a little. She lets out a sigh and closes her eyes. It's not like her to be this quiet.

"I've already started calling around to see if anyone knows of any available places for rent. No one's answering their phones though."

Grandpa snorts and glares over his glasses. "Well Rose, it's barely six in the morning. You have to at least wait until people wake up."

"Why don't you walk down to the convenience store and get a newspaper so we can check the ads. Grab my purse and I'll give you some money."

Gladly.

Chapter Nine

"We have to do something. We can't stay here. Emma has slept on the love seat for over two weeks now. She should be able to sleep in her own bed, in her own room. She will be sixteen in a few months and should be able to have her own space." Gram's not very good at keeping her voice to a whisper but I have to give her credit for trying. It's not like I'm sleeping anyways.

Each day that passes and we are still in this gray house, the circles around my eyes darken more and my migraine intensifies. Pulling the blanket over my head, I roll over and face the back of the couch.

"Mom, we only have one more month before our lease is up. I think we should wait until then so we can get our deposit back. We're going to need that if you want to move. All of those other houses and apartments cost twice as much."

"Deposit? You're worried about that *now*? That went out the window when you let your father tear down the damn wall!" Her voice begins to crack as it always does when she starts to get worked up. "Just think, if you hadn't torn it down, nothing would have happened. I already took care of this once. I don't have it in me to do it again."

"Nothing happened, Rose. They scared themselves. I don't know how many times I have to say it but there's nothing up there."

"Charles, I hear and see everything and sometimes, I think you forget that. The things I heard that night…" *The things she heard.* Why hasn't she said anything about this to me? Which night? "Those are not accepting or welcoming spirits. They want us gone and have made it very clear. Just like…"

"Vroom vroom! Daddy! Let's go outside!" Jake yells as he passes me on his way into the kitchen. Making it so that I can't hear what Gram was about to say. Thanks Jake.

"I'm sorry Jake but I have to go to work. When I get home, we can play outside. Okay buddy?"

Jake starts crying and I take that as my cue to get up.

"Your grandfather is going to Walmart, why don't you go with him." Gram's trying to smile while she's hugging Jake, but I know it's artificial.

"Can I go to work with you today, Dad?" Yeah, school vacations are a much-needed break from school but that means I'm in this house more. I'd much rather spot screws and sweep. Dad's never been an office kind of guy and I'm glad. Jake and I have always enjoyed going to work with Dad and Uncle Troy.

"Your grandmother's going to need your help with Jake today. How about another day?"

"Fine." I want to ask Gram if she's heard back from any of the landlords she has talked to, but she already looks worried and overwhelmed.

"Alright, you guys have a good day and I'll see you when I get home. Love you guys."

"See you later. Be careful and have a good day. Love you too." Gram, Grandpa, and I say in unison. Gram never says good-bye, it's always see you later. Goodbyes are forever and with Gram's superstitions, she says that you should never tell someone goodbye. That's something that has seemed to rub off on the rest of us.

"You know what you're getting at the store right? Maybe Emma should go with you."

"Jake and I can handle it. Your doctor said you shouldn't be left home alone. We will be back in a bit."

After Grams most recent stroke, her doctors have been on high alert. Twice a week there is a visiting nurse that comes to check her vitals and sort her new medications. Every visit the nurse complains about Gram's blood pressure being too high. So of course, that raises it higher than the initial anxiety of the visit. Thankfully, she's not coming today. On the days that she doesn't come, I help Gram with her blood pressure and medication. Before the blood pressure monitor finishes, I already know it's going to be high. Seconds later it beeps a few times, and the display shows that it is in fact higher than recommended.

"You can't write that number down on my chart, Emma."

"Gram, your health is nothing to mess around with. The doctors can't help you if we make up our own numbers to write on your chart and they don't have accurate readings." She used to work in nursing homes, I shouldn't have to remind her of the consequences. Ignoring her, I jot down the numbers that appeared on the little screen. She mumbles something and I ignore that too. Gram is my rock and I'm not about to let anything happen to her. She can be mad all she wants.

By the time we get her morning regimen taken care of and we let Baby outside, Grandpa and Jake are back.

"Emma! Look at what Grandpa won today!" Jake's overly excited and it's hard to see the stuffed animal that he's holding while he jumps up and down. It looks like a teddy bear but I'm not sure. "It's for you!"

"Thank you, Jake and Grandpa!" I may be fifteen, but who doesn't like spontaneous gifts? Grandpa's hands are loaded with gray bags. "Is there anymore in the truck?"

"No, this is it. Out of four games, I won three times today." I swear Grandpa is addicted to the claw machines and he's actually getting quite good at them. "Jake already named it for you."

"Oh really? What's its name?" Jake finally stops hopping around and hands me the light brown teddy bear that I can now see is holding a red heart. He has such an incredible imagination; I can only imagine what he picked. It's probably something like racecar or juice box. He once had a goldfish that he named pudding.

He smiles, "Abigail, but you can call her Abby for short."

My heart drops. "How did you come up with that name?" I haven't told anyone the details of *that* night and there's no way he could have heard us. Besides, that was more than two weeks ago. I doubt he would have remembered.

"We came up with it together!" He says, waving the little red Camaro in my face.

Chapter Ten

"So, when are you guys moving?" Olivia asks as she sits in the chair next to me at the kitchen table. It's been a month since she has come back here, and I can't say I blame her. If I had a choice, I certainly would not come back. Ever.

"Not soon enough." Dad was right, we can't find anywhere big enough for all of us. And with landlords jacking up the cost of rent, most of the rentals are out of our price range.

"How's your Gram doing?"

"The doctors say she should be able to come home in a few days. Her blood pressure has been where they want it for a couple of days now and she's eating. I kind of wish she would stay a little longer because it's a much less stressful place for her and the doctors and nurses are right there if she needs them." I know she worries about all of us when she's not home, but we still visit her daily. After Grandpa drops Jake and I off at school he heads to the nursing home to spend the day with Gram. They may bicker but I can't think of two individuals that love each other more than Gram and Grandpa. After school, Grandpa brings Jake and I to see her for a couple of hours before we have to come home for dinner. Most nights David cooks and for that, I'm grateful.

"Are you ready to go up to your room? My makeup is still in my bag that I left here and if we're going anywhere tonight, I want to do my makeup first."

"About that..." I begin.

"Emma, I promise not to scare you this time."

"I have actually been sleeping in the living room."

"Maybe having Esther up there with you from now on will help you not feel so scared." David joins us in the kitchen and starts digging through the metal cabinet we use as a pantry.

"I'm not scared." *I'm terrified*. "What do you mean from now on?" Esther, David's youngest daughter, lives with her mom and scarcely comes to visit on the weekends. I can't blame her.

"Esther just called me, and she wants to live here so that she can try out a different school. There are some things going on at her current school and her mom isn't planning on moving anytime soon." Oh awesome. As if we didn't already have too many people living with us, making it hard to find a new place to move to. I roll my eyes and David laughs. "Mark my words, you two will be best friends someday."

"Yeah, I doubt that. She's like twelve." I'll admit, she's not as annoying as most kids her age but I'm not going to tell David that.

"Do I need to remind you that you're almost sixteen and are still afraid of the dark? You won't even go upstairs during the day."

"I'm not afraid of the dark, I'm afraid of what's in it. Jerk. Besides, how is a twelve-year-old going to protect anyone?"

"Tell me one person who Esther couldn't make pee their pants." He does have a good point. Esther is also taller than almost everyone her age. I'm almost four years older than her and she's already half a foot taller than me.

"I'm not concerned about people." But maybe this could be slightly more comforting. "When is she moving in?"

"Well, after I figure out what else we need to make dinner, I'm going to go pick her up. You girls want to go?"

"I need to do my makeup still, Emma."

I already know it will take Olivia twenty minutes, easily, to be satisfied with the right shade of eye shadow. "I guess we will stay here." I say even though I have been taking every opportunity that I can to get away from this house.

"You can drive if you want. I'm leaving in ten minutes." I love that David always lets me drive Aunt Karen's Malibu. If I didn't know David, I would assume it was because he didn't want to be seen driving a purple car. But I do know him, and he would drive a bright pink one if given the chance.

"Alright Olivia, chop chop!" I say while clapping my hands. Since Uncle Troy and David have started teaching me how to drive, I don't pass up any prospect of practicing. I want to be prepared to take my driving test so that I can pass as soon as I'm able to take it. I can't wait for that freedom. Freedom away from this house. Hopefully we won't still be living here by the time I get my license though.

"If you want me to hurry up, then we need to go upstairs to get my makeup."

As much as I don't want to go up there, I do really want to drive. I take a deep breath. "Alright, let's go. But you're going first."

"Alright, fine."

Reaching the bottom of the stairs, my heart starts racing. *I can do this. I can do this.* I close my eyes as my hand grasps the wooded banister. With each step, my hand continues to slide up the dusty banister and my eyes stay closed. This way, I can't see anything.

"Well, the creepy room door is still closed."

"That's good." I whisper and continue down the hall towards my room. Only opening one eye slightly to verify that the door is in fact closed, and it is. Luckily, the old wooden banister keeps going all the way to my room, so I keep my eyes closed. Once my hand bumps against the wall, I finally open my eyes. My room is just how we left it. The makeshift ouija board folder is still on the middle of my floor surrounded by candles. Quickly, I put the candles back on the black wire rack and crumple up the folder so that it fits into the small trash bag. I go over to where my necklace landed, after flying against the wall but it's not there.

"Olivia, did you pick up my necklace?"

"No, I'm busy trying to get my makeup done. It's not on the floor?"

"I don't see it." Crouching down, I check under the couch and TV stand but it's not there. My dresser is on the other side of the room. I doubt it would be under there, but I'll check anyways. "Yeah, I don't see it anywhere." I say and grip the dresser to pull myself up. Directly at eye level, the little silver teddy bear is dangling from a hook in my jewelry box. "What the hell, Olivia! I thought you said you hadn't seen it?"

"I haven't." Setting the small brush in her hand down, she turns towards me, and her eyes are quick to focus on the little teddy bear. "Maybe someone came up here and put it away. It wasn't me though."

"That's not possible. No one's been up here since that night."

"Girls, I'm leaving!" David yells from the bottom of the stairs. He won't admit it, but I think he's too afraid to come up here now.

Since I know David is waiting at the bottom of the stairs, I don't bother closing my eyes to head back downstairs. As hard as I try not to look down that hall, something catches my attention out of the corner of my eye. That damn door is open again.

Chapter Eleven

"Why is there nothing good playing on the radio?" Aunt Karen always has the best CDs, so I reach under the passenger seat and pull out the overstuffed black case. "Olivia, what do you want to listen to?"

"Does your aunt have the new Now album?"

Sure enough, she does and it's right on top when I let the case fall open on my lap. "Now 66?" I'm not as up to date on new releases. Aside from a few CD's, I usually just listen to the radio in my bedroom. Well, in my old bedroom anyways.

"Yes, that one!"

Patiently, I wait for whatever CD that's already in the player to eject. Abruptly, my door swings open and as I whip my head around, Esther is climbing in, and her arms are wrapped tight, too tight around me.

"Emma! I've missed you!" I feel like I'm being suffocated and recollections of that night with the ouija board come back.

Black eyes.

I can't breathe.

Space. I need space.

"Get off of me!" I yell and push as hard as I can against Esther's shoulders. Finally, she climbs back out and I fight the urge to cry.

"What's your problem?"

Still fighting the tears, I shake my head. "I just don't want to be touched."

"Okay then!" She shouts as she climbs into the backseat behind me, and I turn around so that I can see her. Rolling her eyes, she blows the long piece of hair off her face and slumps against the seat.

The trunk slams shut, shaking the car. "Everything alright girls?" David asks as he sits into the driver seat next to me.

"Well, I went to give Emma a hug and she got all bitchy for no reason."

"Esther! Watch your mouth. Emma, what's the matter?"

"Just don't touch me and I'll be fine." Soon she will see why. Not that I would wish for anyone to experience the gray house, but she's already made the choice to move. Unlike me, she got to choose her fate. Also, unlike me if she doesn't like it, she can just move back with her mom.

"So, you really want to live in a real-life haunted house, huh?" I hate talking about the house but at least Olivia's question takes the spotlight off me.

"Jesus Olivia, do you really need to mention that right now? Esther has barely buckled up." David's over exaggerating. Olivia waited a solid five minutes before saying anything. That's longer than I expected her to wait.

"Dad, what's Olivia talking about?"

"Nothing don't worry about it. Emma, why don't I pull over and you can drive?"

I shake my head. I know this is his way to distract me. I'm usually fairly quiet when I'm driving. I drove the forty-five minutes to this quaint Vermont town; he can drive now. Besides, I'm pretty sure I'm only legally allowed to drive with one person over the age of twenty-five.

"Esther, you won't believe what happened to us! Have you seen the creepy room yet?" Olivia is practically bouncing off her seat.

Esther shrugs her shoulders. "If you guys are trying to scare me, it's not going to happen. And no, I haven't been over for like two months."

David grins, clearly impressed with his daughter. "As I said on the phone there are a few rooms you can chose from. The one above the kitchen is cool. I told Emma that she should have picked that one."

"Why didn't you?" Esther asks in a rather sassy tone, and I contemplate even answering her. She will find out soon enough. Should I attempt to tell her the real reason?

"I just liked mine better." That's not a lie. I like any room better than that one.

The rest of the way home is anything but quiet. Esther fills David in on everything happening at her mom's. Olivia sings along with the whole Now CD, and I just try to rack my brain about what to do with this moving situation. Finding a place for five people is hard enough, never mind eight.

At last, David pulls into the driveway and I'm the first to hop out of the car. I just need a few minutes of quiet before I lose it. Besides the TV, our old house was always quiet. Since moving here, there is always noise. Obnoxious cars and trucks are always driving by. Someone is always talking. A minimum of two TV's are always blaring at any given time. When Baby is awake, she's usually growling. And if by some miracle it is quiet, the house creaks and the *others* who still live here make it known that they are restless and unhappy. I'm over it and I'm beginning to wonder just how much more I can handle.

The barn door is open, meaning that Grandpa is in the barn stripping wire or crushing cans. For my sanity, I hope he's just stripping wire.

"What are you up to, Emmy?" Grandpa's cigar wiggles between his lips when he talks and the ashes fall between his legs, just barely missing the white bucket he's clipping bare copper wire into.

"I just need somewhere quiet for a little bit." I begin glancing around the barn for a corner or somewhere to hide. Three of the five horse stalls are stuffed with junk from the previous tenants. The other two are empty but I can't bring myself to sit where there once was horse crap.

"You've come to the right place. Pull that chair over and take a seat." My eyes follow Grandpa's cigar that he uses to point with, and I notice a green camping chair leaning against the wall. Above it there's an old, weathered poster. "Can you read what that says?" He asks.

"It looks like an old ad for a horse stable. Two dollars per night?" The longer I'm in here, the more I'm amazed with how calm it is.

"Two dollars? Yeah, I'd say that's pretty old. You can't get anything for two dollars nowadays."

"Sure, you can, Grandpa." With one shake, the chair pops open.

"Not like you used to though." Nothing's like it used to be according to Gram and Grandpa. The last time Gram sent me to get her a package of Necco Wafers, she couldn't believe that they cost almost a dollar. Back in her day, she paid five cents.

"There you are Emma! We're about to go upstairs. Are you coming?"

I slouch in the camping chair, it's quite comfortable. If only they let me be for five more minutes, I could easily fall asleep right here. "Do I have a choice?"

"Nope. Let's go." Olivia and Esther each grab one of my arms and drag me along.

Grandpa chuckles, "I'll see you girls later."

Without me having to suggest it, Olivia goes first up the stairs. Esther follows and I continue to drag my feet behind them.

"Which room is yours?"

"Mine's over there." I point my finger behind me, but my eyes stay focused on the floor. This seems like a safe place to look.

"Look at this purple! I'm not a huge fan of purple but it's better than the boring white walls that I'm used to."

"The one across the hall is pink if you'd rather have a pink room. We just painted it a couple weeks ago." Olivia suggests.

I forgot about that dark spot until she just mentioned us painting. With one quick glance, the dark spot is still there. Only now it's darker than before.

"Ew. No thank you. And there's no window? Next." After a few steps, Esther stops. I don't have to look up to know that she's staring at the creepy room. "Well, that room looks creepy as..."

"Yeah, we can keep moving." I push past them. My luck, whatever resides in that room will grab me and pull me in there, slamming the door behind. We are fully aware that it can forcefully open and close that door. I have no interest to see what *else* it is capable of.

"Woah dude! Check out this floor! It's so red, and I bet if you swept up the dust, you could use the floor as a mirror. I've never seen a floor so shiny. With all of these rooms up here, why are you the only one that moved up here?" Good question.

"Everyone's too afraid I guess."

"Besides *that* room over there, I think it's awesome up here! Can I see your room?"

"Yeah, come in." I push the door open and step aside.

"This is awesome! Can we just share a room? At least until I have stuff to put in my own room?"

Share a room? I've never shared a room with anyone. Older siblings that have to share with younger siblings usually complain and fight about sharing rooms. Esther isn't my sister though. Maybe it could work for a little while. That way, maybe I won't be so terrified. "Okay, but only until you have stuff for your room."

"This is going to be awesome!" Once again, her arms are around me and I want to scream. When I start to push at her shoulders again, she let's go and steps back. "Oh, I'm so sorry."

I need to set some boundaries. "There's one rule though."

"I promise not to touch your stuff." Esther's voice is loud like her dads but only when she's overly excited or angry. I think I can handle that.

"I appreciate it, but I don't care if you use my stuff. Just make sure you put it back."

"Okay, then what's the rule?"

"Do. Not. Touch. Me." The words come out slowly, just as I intended them too in hopes that she will take them as seriously as I mean them. Because if she doesn't, this arrangement isn't going to work.

Chapter Twelve

"Did you pick a room, Esther?" David asks as we start stacking our dinner bowls in the sink.

"Yeah, the purple one but Emma said I can share her room until I get mine set up." I find it amusing that each room seems to be referred to by color.

David stops mid bite and looks at me. "Really? And Emma, you're okay with that?"

"It's only short term." When I say short term, I mean two weeks max. My definition of short term is obviously different than everyone else's that lives here.

"Okay. I'm going to find some yard sales in the morning if you girls would like to come. Tomorrow is the big Charlestown yard sale."

"Sure." Esther and I answer.

I love yard sales. Gram and one of her sister's used to bring me all the time when I was little. I remember those two crazy ladies carrying a decent sized couch home. I'm not sure how far we had to walk but at the time it felt like forever. Her sister had suggested that we leave it right there on the side of the road until Grandpa got home and then he could pick it up with his truck. Gram laughed, stomped out her cigarette and said, "We have to get it home before Charles gets home from work. That way he can't say no. Now, pick up your side and hurry up!" That was back before she got sick. Speaking of Gram, she should be home any day now. Maybe I can find something for her.

"Hey Dad! Emma and Olivia are going for a walk to Walmart. Can I go with them?"

"If they want you to go, that's fine with me." I appreciate that he's not forcing us to hang out.

I shrug my shoulders. "It's something to do and it gets us out of this house."

"Here's a few dollars. Make sure you girls are back within two hours." David knows we could easily spend the remainder of the night at Walmart. Especially since you can now play Guitar Hero in the game section. Who can say no to Pat Benatar? It beats staying in this creepy house.

"Emma, don't you know a few of those guys?" Olivia stops just as we get halfway through the entryway at Walmart.

"What guys?" Glancing around the entrance, I only see an older woman with a little boy that she's trying to buckle into the cart. The little boy is not having it and he keeps standing. That can't be who she's referring to though.

"The ones in Dunkin Donuts, sitting right in front of your face?"

Spotting the group, there is a few that I recognize. Of course, it's easy to see who it is since they noticed us first and are now staring. The tallest one, Jay waves for us to join. By the time we reach them, they have pulled three more chairs up to their already overfilled table.

"What are you ladies up to?" Jay asks and all eyes remain on us.

My hands begin to feel clammy, and I try to take a deep breath. I hate groups of people. I always freeze during class presentations. Recently, I figured out that if I forget the assignment at home, I can just hand it in late and bypass standing in front of the class. Yeah, that lowers my grade since the presentation is usually half of it but if I don't have to be the center of attention, it's fine with me. Even though I know Jay and Simon, I have no idea who the other three are. They look younger though so that's probably why.

"We're going to play Guitar Hero, obviously." Esther doesn't sit and neither do I. Olivia picks one of the chairs that they pulled up.

"What are you guys doing?" Compared to their rowdiness when we walked in, my voice hardly comes out as a whisper. Thankfully, they are all quiet now, so I don't have to repeat myself.

"Just taking a break. We rode our bikes here." Jay straightens in the metal chair, appearing even taller.

"From your house? Isn't that like ten miles?" I can't help but feel concerned. What if someone hits them or kidnaps them? Oh god, I sound like my grandmother. I'm not sure if that's good or bad. "Are you riding them back too?"

"Yeah probably. We do it all the time." Simon answers like it's no big deal.

"We have to get headed back soon but we can come back tomorrow if you ladies want to hang out."

Normally I would say no, but this would get us out of the house for the rest of tomorrow. A whole day spent anywhere else sounds wonderful. "Maybe tomorrow afternoon? We have plans in the morning."

"I'm Esther by the way!" Esther playfully pushes on my shoulder. "Thanks for introducing me."

"Oh, Esther. This is Jay, Simon and..." I pause and hope someone else can finish since I'm still just as clueless as to who the others are.

"Damon, Holden and Martin." Jay points to each of them and finishes the introduction.

"Imagine if we had boxes for arms?" Holden says while waving an empty Ring Ding box around on his arm, knocking over a few bottles of water in his wake.

My big sister instinct kicks in. "Hey Ring Ding, you should probably be a little more careful. Maybe that's why we don't have boxes for arms." My outburst surprises me and apparently everyone else, but just for a brief moment and then laughter fills the small coffee shop.

"Ring Ding! That's awesome. Can we go now?" Esther is getting impatient and I'm ready to go too. That's enough socializing for me for today.

"Bye everyone." Olivia's chair screeches across the tiled floor, like nails on a chalk board, as she returns it to an empty table and we all cringe.

"See you guys later." I quickly say as Esther tugs at my arm.

"Bye Ring Ding!" Esther yells from outside the coffee shop.

After an hour of Guitar Hero, we headed back the gray house. Most people would refer to their house as "home" but not me. This house has never felt like home and never will.

Upstairs, Olivia, Esther and I congregate in my room. Esther has made herself comfortable on my bed, thankfully she brought her own blankets. Olivia's laying in a pile of blankets and pillows on the floor. She claims it's comfortable, but it doesn't look like it to me. After starting the movie, I crawl under my blankets and Tiggy cuddles up next to me.

Aunt Karen is not only up to date with the latest music, but she also has all the newest DVDs. Tonight, we picked Talladega Nights to watch first. If we make it through, John Tucker is next. For the first time since we moved in, tonight actually feels normal. Well, except for the ceiling light, lamp and two nightlights that are on. It's not that I'm afraid of the dark, I'm afraid of what's in it.

Soon after the movie begins, Esther and Olivia are oddly quiet. Sitting up slightly, I can see they are both sleeping. Must be nice. It's still weird to me that I'm not the first one to fall asleep anymore. I lay back down and close my eyes. I can only hope that sleep will come soon.

Just as I start to fall asleep, I feel like I'm falling into a hole and my body twitches, causing me to wake up. I hate those dreams.

Next to me, Tiggy stirs and eventually stands. He's not like normal cats, he doesn't terrorize the house in the middle of the night. When I lay down, he stays with me until I get up. Only I'm not getting up. Matter of fact, I'm comfortable. Or at least I *was*.

But now, his ears start twitching as he glares intently at my bedroom door. It's closed and barricaded with my heavy dresser. There's no way it can *blow* open tonight. I close my eyes and try to fall back asleep. Tonight, *will* be a normal night.

Tiggy starts hissing and the doorknob starts rattling. I inhale slowly and try to think of all the other people that it could possibly be.

"Dad?" No answer.

"Jake?" No answer.

"Grandpa?" No answer.

"David?" No answer.

One of them would have answered by now. I know they would have. The rattling quickens and the door begins to jiggle with such force that my dresser starts to move.

"LEAVE ME THE FUCK ALONE!" Everything stills. Except for Esther and Olivia, who are finally waking up. Tiggy jumps on the floor and starts clawing at the door casing while making a growling sound. I had no idea a cat could make a sound so spine-chilling.

"Woah." Esther rubs her eyes and sits up. "Emma, what's going on?"

"Did I fall asleep?" Olivia's eyes dart to the TV and the credit are scrolling. "I missed the whole movie?"

Unexpectedly, there is a thunderous thud against the door, and we all jump.

Esther bravely climbs off the bed and begins to move the dresser. Olivia scrambles to her feet and leaps onto my bed.

So much for a normal sleepover. So much for finally getting some much-needed sleep.

"Uh... What are you doing Esther?" My whole body trembles. Part of me wants to stop her, but the other part wants to see what will happen if I don't. Will she see what I see? Will it attack her like it has me?

"I'm going to see who's rudely banging on the door! That's what I'm going to do! And before you say it's a ghost, just know that I'm not afraid of them either." Swiftly, she yanks the door open, and her jaw drops.

Chapter Thirteen

When Esther doesn't move, I start to panic. Is someone other than Aunt Karen finally seeing what I see? Doubtful. Otherwise, she would be screaming by now. Tiggy bolts into the hallway, continuing that awful growling sound. I can feel the hairs standing up on the back of my neck and goosebumps traveling down my arms. I can't sit here in suspense any longer.

"What is it, Esther?" Still, she doesn't answer, and I cautiously make my way towards her. Am I really prepared to see whatever it is that she's looking at? Halfway there, she starts stepping into the hallway. It can't be too bad if she's walking towards it, right?

"Is that blood running down the wall?" Her voice is shaky. In the nearly ten years that I have known Esther, I've never seen her scared. Until now.

Vigilantly, I step into the hallway and look ahead. My breath catches as dark red liquid seeps down the aged white wall. "That was *not* there when we got home." At this point, I wouldn't be the least bit surprised if it were blood.

"I definitely would have noticed that." I think all of us would have.

"What is that?" Olivia asks as she emerges from my bedroom.

Esther disappears into the purple room. "Dad! Please tell me this isn't blood running down the wall up here!" It takes me a moment to realize she is yelling through the vent in the floor. Finally, a good use for those.

Seconds later David is running up the stairs. "What do you mean blood?"

"Right there Dad! You see that, right?"

"Oh. Um... you know, I'm not really sure what that is." He's shaking his head but the worry in his eyes doesn't match. "It's not blood though."

"Oh, no? Then please enlighten us as to what it could be, David."

"Well, this is an old house." He starts. "There might be a leak in the roof."

"A leak in the roof? That's the best you've got, Dad? If that were the case, don't you think it would be clear or maybe even tinted brown?"

"There *should* be a liner in the chimney but that doesn't necessarily mean there is one. It could be soot seeping through."

"The furnace is all the way in the basement. What you're saying is the 'soot' is somehow rising this high and just happens to be seeping not only through the bricks *and* cement but *also* through the wood lathe wall, plaster, *and* paint? We're not even using the heat right now!"

David scratches his forehead and glares at the wall once again.

"Awesome. What else has to happen for us to move out of here? The damn walls are bleeding! And here you are fabricating some bullshit excuse!"

"Emma, that's not blood." His voice is low and distracted as his eyes are glued to the wall. I think he's trying to convince himself, not us.

"When the roof collapses and buries us all alive, you will all wish that you would have listened to me sooner." Stomping back to my room, the collar on my favorite purple hooded long sleeve shirt suddenly feels tighter. Pulling at it to stretch it out does nothing, it just keeps tightening after I let go. I've had this shirt for about two years now and this has never been a problem. When I glance in the mirror, I expect to see someone bunching up the hood, causing it to continue tightening, but no one is there. The strings look relaxed as they always are. As it tightens more, I can see the stitching starting to stretch as it starts to dig into my throat, making it harder to breathe. Grabbing the bottom hem, I rip if over my head, but the collar gets stuck, and it takes a few tugs to finally get if completely off. Still struggling to take a full breath, I do my best to ease myself to sit on the floor. The shirt is a few feet away from me, but it still feels like I'm wearing it. My hands franticly feel my neck for anything else that may be constricting. They freeze when I feel a delicate cold chain.

I wasn't wearing a necklace. I haven't worn a necklace in a year or so.

As quick as I can, I find the small clasp. It's too tiny to grasp and keeps slipping out of my fingertips.

"Give in." A gravelly voice reverberates through me as the necklace tightens more.

I refuse to die in this house and be trapped here forever. Gripping the thin chain is hard since it only makes it tighter but finally my fingers make it between my throat and the necklace. After a couple good tugs, it breaks free. Little pieces of the chain ting against the wall and dresser. At last, I can breathe.

Looking down at my still clenched fist, I open it, revealing the little teddy bear holding the pink stone. The same necklace that we used for the ouija board. Also, the same necklace that we couldn't find earlier. I only remember wearing this a handful of times as a child. There's no way I would wear it now. How did it get around my neck in the first place? Where did it come from?

Chapter Fourteen

"We're here girls. Are you planning on sleeping in the car all day or are you actually going to get up and check out some yard sales?" David's loud voice wakes me up and I nudge Esther, who is still asleep next to me. Neither of us slept last night. We ended up cutting the collars off all my shirts while Olivia slept.

"Don't start with me David." I glare at him, and he laughs, frustrating me even more. "What's so funny?"

"I've been preparing myself for the teenage girl attitudes since Esther's mom found out we were having a second girl. So, go ahead and be mad at the world. I won't take it personally."

"Oh, I'm not mad at the world." I argue.

"Dad, just stop. Before that house murders one of us, we should move." Finally, someone is on my side.

"Not you too, Esther. Emma's just overthinking everything."

"Overthinking? Do you think she tried choking herself?"

• • •

"Well of course not but…"

"Let's get this over with." I say as I get out of the car, slamming the door behind me.

The yard sale event is quite impressive. I've gone to yard sales with Gram before but never a whole town wide yard sale. At some yellow cape style house with white trim, I found the perfect set of earrings for Gram. In the sunlight, the diamond like stones sparkle and I can't wait to give them to her. Normally, I wouldn't buy something like earrings at a yard sale because, well that's kind of gross. But this particular pair is still in the package and has never been worn.

David found Esther a dresser and nightstand, along with several other things that he claims are a *great find*. I'm not sure why he would ever need old baseball gloves or some decorative teapot but whatever makes him happy. Esther picked up a DVD player so that she will now have one in her room. The sellers weren't sure if it actually worked, so they gave it to her for free.

Once we're back in the car, I send Jay a message to let him know we will be back soon if they still want to hang out. I could use the distraction and some more time away from that house. Epically after last night. Immediately, I receive a text back saying that they are already in town.

"What are you girls doing this afternoon?" David asks.

"Olivia is supposed to come back over. Actually, can we stop and pick her up?"

"That's the one that lives by the cemetery?"

"Odd landmark to choose but yeah." Olivia also lives by a gas station, a doctor's office, and a school, but he chooses a cemetery? Okay.

"And then what are you girls doing?"

"Nosey much? I think anything we do is safer than staying at the house."

Esther clears her throat. "We should go to the park Emma."

"Okay." I text Jay back to see if they want to meet us at one of the many parks in town.

"Who else will be at the park?"

"How am I supposed to know? It's a public park." What is this, twenty questions?

"Who are you texting?"

"Dad! How about you give Emma some privacy. You're not her dad."

"Okay fine but you better not be doing anything you're not supposed to be doing. Karen and I might swing down to the park and watch the game later." Even though David doesn't come out and say it, we already know this is his way of warning us that he will be watching. Too bad they didn't feel this protective while we are at the house.

Jay, Simon and his cousin are waiting on the bleachers when we get to the park. Before we can reach the door handles David starts his twenty questions again.

"Who are these guys and how old are they?"

"Just friends and they are my age." I answer.

"Does your grandmother know them?"

"Well, they've had the *pleasure* of speaking to her on the phone a few times." I say sarcastically.

They are some of the few friends that have dared to continue to call me on the house phone after Gram interrogated them. Most are too intimidated to call back. I remember one time, I asked her if Collin and Preston could come over and she actually agreed. To say I was shocked would be the understatement of the century. When they got there, I thought she was sleeping. As they walked by, she sat up and asked, "Where are your fucking jackets?" As soon as it hits sixty degrees, she's always nagging everyone to wear jackets. That day it was in the twenties, so she was furious. Anyways, they were so scared to walk past her again that they jumped out of my bedroom window. Which due to the hill, my window was about a story and a half from the ground. She was convinced that they were still in my room a week later.

"Well alright then." David knows all too well how Gram is.

Chapter Fifteen

"What happened to your shirt and your neck?" Jay and Simon ask. Before I can say anything, Olivia starts filling them in and doesn't stop until she tells them everything.

"I don't believe in ghosts. I'll go in the so-called creepy room." Simon mocks.

Olivia smiles and I already know what she's thinking before she says it. "I'll go with you!" She's relentless.

"Alright, let's go then." Simon jumps off the bleachers and waits for us to do the same.

Jay's hesitant when Esther and I don't follow. "It really can't be that bad, can it?"

"Yes, it can." I say, which causes my throat to hurt even more. My hand traces the black and blue around my neck from last night and I'm reminded of just how bad it can be. "Olivia made it seem more like a dream than the nightmare that it is." Esther nods her head in agreement with me.

"We won't let anything bad happen to any of you." Jay promises. I know he means well but I also know that's not a promise that he can make. Until they experience firsthand the evil of that house, their opinions and promises are invalid.

"I don't think you know what you're up against." Esther cuts in.

"Stop being scaredy cats! Let's go!" Simon's now kicking at the grass as he paces in front of the bleachers.

"I was actually looking forward to sometime away from that place today." I whisper in attempt to not hurt my throat anymore, but that's not much better. It still hurts. I'm still stunned that the dainty chain didn't break before I pulled at it.

"Me too and I just moved in." The fact that Esther is scared makes me even more alert.

"You know what? Esther and I will hang out here. You can all go if you want. Olivia can show you around. I'm sure she would be more than happy to."

That gets Simon's attention, and he stills. "What? We can't just go hang out at your house without you being there."

"It's not my house." I want so badly to yell but it hardly comes out as a whisper. "It's also nowhere I would want to *hang out*."

"But you live there. It would be awkward if we were there, and you weren't." It will be awkward either way.

"We could wait outside." Jay suggests but then adds, "Simon, maybe this isn't a good idea."

"Come on, Jay. Don't leave me hanging now!"

"Alright, fine. You guys want to see it so bad, then let's go." As Esther jumps off the metal bleachers, I'm left sitting there in shock.

"Seriously?" Taking my time, I step down and follow them through the park. Unfortunately, we decided to meet at the park closest to the house. Right now, I'm wishing that someone had suggested the one at the other end of town. Then maybe this idea wouldn't have even surfaced.

The closer we get, the more my hands shake, and my legs weaken with each step.

Sirens are in the distance and by the sounds of it, they are headed in our direction. We're about five minutes away and I look ahead, secretly hoping to see the gray house up in flames. But it's not. It's still standing there, staring back at me. Waiting for its next victim. And here the six of us are, walking into it. Creating our own misery.

"Oh, so spooky." Simon continues to mock, waving his arms around.

Esther leans closer to me, but not too close. I know she comes from a family of huggers, but I couldn't be more relieved that she is starting to be conscious of my space. "Can I like punch him in the face?"

I nod my head and Jay chuckles. "Please do."

It may be almost seven but with summer almost here, there is still a few more hours of daylight left. If this were a horror movie, a group of six teens and preteens would be fine because it's still sunny out. But this isn't a horror movie. This is my real-life nightmare, and we already know whatever haunts the gray house doesn't care if it's night or day.

"Finally, someone will go into that room with me! I can't wait to check it out again." Olivia's fascination with this room is getting old. I'm starting to wonder if there's something more.

"I'm not scared to go with you."

"We know. That's what you keep saying." Jay answers and rolls his eyes. "Are you trying to convince yourself or us?"

"I don't need to convince myself of anything." Simon's arrogance makes me want to punch him in the face. "Emma, can we say hi to Gram?"

"*My* Gram is still in the nursing home. She should be home in a couple of days."

Olivia leads the way up the stairs and in a single file, we follow behind. The stairs creak louder than usual, intensifying the already unnerving feeling. It's just from the extra weight and stress on the old wood. I hope.

"Emma, is that blood running down the wall?" Everyone, including Simon stops.

"Yep." Esther confirms and takes the next step.

"You're just trying to mess with us, aren't you?" Simon accuses but remains standing on the same step.

No need to, the house will. I want to say but I'm too afraid to. Olivia and Simon are surely going to irritate the ghosts enough. I'll just keep my thoughts to myself. It's safer that way.

"Who's the scaredy cat now?" Standing at the top of the stairs with her hands on her hips, Esther easily towers over Simon. For a second, I expected him to take off back down the stairs.

Olivia grips the doorknob to the creepy room and pauses. "Are you ready, Simon?"

"Of course, what are you waiting for?" Running up the last few steps, he joins her.

Silently, we watch the door swing open. The wallpaper has continued to peel but the teddy bear poster is still holding up. From what I can see, the room looks empty. For now, anyways.

Gram always says that spirts only show themselves if they know you're ready to see them. I used to believe that but not so much anymore. Never in my lifetime would I be ready to see the things that I have seen in this house.

Esther, Jay, Simon's cousin, and I keep our distance by staying at the entrance to the narrow hallway. I refuse to venture any closer. I still can't figure out what exactly happened the last time when everything went black.

"What's up with the eyes on this crawl space door?"

"Woah. That was NOT here the last time I came in here. Emma, come check this out!" Olivia shouts.

Should I? No. I should stay right here. Far away from that room. I don't care to see what they are talking about. Somethings are better left unseen and I'm sure this qualifies as one.

"Emma!" She shouts. "I bet Abigail drew this for us! Remember when we asked her to draw us a picture?"

"You." I correct. "You asked her to draw a picture. I'm good though. I'll take your word for it." Someone's hand presses against my back, pushing me down the hallway. When I turn to see who it is, there's no one directly behind me. Esther's hands are in her pockets. Simon's cousin is sitting on the stairs picking at his shoes. Jay is leaning against one of the walls with his arms crossed in front of him. *Who is touching me?*

"I think we should check out what's behind here. Maybe the *ghosts* wanted to get your attention." I hear Simon say quietly to Olivia as I get closer to the door.

"I bet you're right." Olivia has her hopes up and I feel bad because Simon's just being a sarcastic...

"Okay, that's seriously creepy!" Footsteps are coming towards me, and I can hear Simon and Olivia talking but I can't make out what they are saying anymore.

Everything has gone black again. I try to step backwards but the pressure against my back is more forceful than before. So forceful that I expect to tumble forward down into the creepy room, but something is holding me up. It feels almost like a glass door. It's even cool to the touch. With nowhere else to go, panic takes over. I try stepping to the side but the only place that takes me is up against another wall.

I need to get out of here.

Wait a second. As my hands trace across the cool surface, I realize that it's actually the door to the red room. Following the trim down to the doorknob, I turn it quickly and fall face first onto the glossy red floor.

"Emma!"

The air is heavy, making it hard to breathe. Voices echo around me as I try to open my eyes, but they feel too heavy.

"Let's get her off the floor." *Who is that?*

"Trust me, don't touch her. Just give her a few minutes." That sounds like Esther, but her voice is much lower than usual.

My head starts pounding and it feels like the floor beneath me is spinning. Suddenly, something moves under my shoulders and behind my knees. When I no longer feel the floor under me, my eyes fly open and all I see is more blood running down the walls.

"Put me down!" I shriek.

Chapter Sixteen

Still unaware of who's carrying me, all I can see is the blood running down the wall of the red room. My eyes follow the streams, all the way down to the glossy red floor where it is dripping into a dark red puddle. Several inches above the floor, it has begun to splatter the white walls. This isn't from the chimney. It can't be.

"Emma! Are you okay?" When my eyes open again, Olivia's face is too close to mine. The distance between us is just enough room for her to wave her hand back and forth while she continues to snap her fingers.

"Can you back up?" Thankfully, she does and I'm able to glance around. Jay, Simon, his cousin, and Esther are still here, and we are now in my bedroom. My head is still pounding. How did we get in here? Dipping my head, I attempt to relieve some tension by massaging my forehead and temples. On the left side of my forehead is a sizeable lump. Did I really fall that hard? If so, it's no wonder as to why my head is pounding.

"*Get out of her face.*" Grams familiar voice comes from beside me.

Hold on.

Am I hearing things? Gram isn't due home for another day or so. What day is it? Is it still Saturday? How long did I black out for? There's no way that she would be able to come up here. I scan the floor for Gram's green oxygen hose, but I don't see it. Wherever she goes, the hose follows.

She's not actually here. I assure myself.

"*I know you can hear me.*" Gram's voice continues and I try my hardest not to look beside me. I must have hit my head harder than I thought. Maybe I have a concussion.

Taking a deep breath, I try to block it out. I need something else to focus on. Gradually, I look up from the gray painted floor and Simon's grinning ear to ear. He's holding something in his hands, but I can't figure out what it is. "Simon, what are you holding?"

"*The key to the door.*" A deep growl reverberates from the same direction that Gram's voice came from just moments ago. I inhale sharply as a chill runs down my spine.

What door? Still too afraid to look next to me, I keep my eyes focused straight ahead. Simon opens his hands, and I can finally make out what he's holding. Cradled in his hands is a skull. "Uh. Please tell me I'm just seeing things. Where the hell did you get that?"

"Well, you did fall pretty hard. How's your head feeling?" Olivia asks and I chose to ignore her too. I appreciate her concern but what kind of question is that? Obviously, it doesn't feel too great.

"You know, the crawl space door? The one with the two eyes drawn on it? That you three are convinced that some ghost chick drew?"

"One of the eyes are blood shot." Olivia adds.

"I'm not sure what this skull belongs to, but it looks pretty cool! Doesn't it? Oh, and you lied to me! Gram's downstairs, I just showed her, and I think I made her mad." He says as he shrugs his shoulders.

"*The key*." Oh man. "You have to put that back. Right now!"

"That's what I said." Standing as far away from Simon as she can, Esther is sitting on the floor, tugging at a string on her shirt.

"Did you say you showed *my* Gram? That's not possible, Gram's not here. She won't be until tomorrow at the earliest." Now I'm really confused. I guess I did fall hard.

"Yes, she is. I just walked past her on my way back up here after using the bathroom. Not even kidding."

Without saying a word to anyone, I run out of my room and into the hall. Standing in the doorway to the small pink room is an older man. The sight of him catches me off guard and stops me in my tracks. I feel like I've seen him before. The way the sun is shining as it sets through the purple room window, makes him appear almost translucent, just like Abigail. As he starts towards me, the sound of chains clang behind him and I run down the stairs. I reach the bottom and glance out the little window in the door, hoping to see Grandpa's truck but all I see are two little feet and a white dress standing at the top of the stairs behind me. I blink a few times but she's still there.

Finally, I reach the living room and Gram is sitting on the couch. I'm hesitant to get too close. How do I know if this is really Gram this time? If it is her, then Grandpa should be here too, but he's not. He wouldn't just leave her here without telling me. Would he? Maybe he didn't know we were here.

"You better tell your friend to go put that back where he found it." When Baby jumps up next to her and starts licking her face, I start to relax.

"Yes Gram, that's what I told him."

"How many boys are up there? Did you ask your grandfather if they could come over?"

"I'm sorry Gram. They are leaving in a few minutes. They let you leave early?"

"They needed the bed for someone else. Is this what you do when I'm not here? Have boys over and snoop around, getting into things you know damn well to leave be?" She pauses to catch her breath. "Have any of the landlords called back?"

"Not yet." I wish they would. Oftentimes when I pass by the living room phone, I pick it up to make sure it still works. I can't afford to miss any calls.

"Don't worry. I'll find us somewhere else."

"I know you will, Gram."

"Come over here and let me give you a kiss on your forehead before you take off again." Everyone starts running down the stairs and I bend down to give Gram a quick hug.

"You put that back, right?" Gram glares over her glasses at Simon.

"Yes ma'am."

Gram hates being called ma'am. I wait for her to throw something at him, but she doesn't. Maybe this isn't Gram. When she mumbles a few colorful words, any doubt vanishes. This is my Gram.

"Where's Grandpa?" I ask before we head outside. I don't want to leave her alone after everything I just saw. I know Gram will see them too and she surely doesn't need the stress. Not that me being here will change anything. This last year, I feel like I'm the main cause of her stress and that makes me feel terrible. If I had known that she was going to be home, I wouldn't have let anyone over, not even Olivia. Not because I have anything to hide, because I don't. I learned a few years ago that Gram always finds everything out. Company just makes her more stressed, and I can see why.

"He just went to pick up my medicine. He should be back in a few minutes." She's glaring over her glasses again but she's not looking at Simon anymore. She's looking in the direction of the hallway to the stairs.

From where I'm standing, I don't have to turn my head to see the little girl in the white dress. As her eyes scan the room, she looks disoriented. Somethings off about her. Each time I see her I notice something different, or maybe I'm just noticing more details. Her face is still pale, much like a porcelain doll. The once white dress is still tattered. There are still no shoes on her little bare feet. Her hands though, how did I not notice that her right hand doesn't have any fingers? My focus swiftly shifts to her left hand that is tracing the dusty rose colored living room wall, there is no index finger.

I quickly glance at everyone, but I must have been so intrigued by what's in front of me that I didn't notice that they moved to the kitchen.

"Never have I been down here before." Her voice is a faint whisper.

"What do you want?" Gram's whisper catches me off guard since she's not usually one to whisper this quietly.

As the little girl turns to face us, a cold breeze blows gently through the room. "To keep you safe."

"From what?" Gram's voice raises slightly, and I know her blood pressure is rising.

Just as her head tilts up to the ceiling and her ratty hair falls down her back, there is a loud thud upstairs followed by a horrific bellowing scream.

"Him."

Chapter Seventeen

My eyes dart to the celling as the terrifying thuds continue across the red room floor above us. It seriously sounds just like someone is stomping, only everyone is now outside, and Gram and I are left in here by ourselves.

What if *he* can now come downstairs too? It's clear that Abigail hasn't been down here until now. What if that skull actually was a key of some sort, trapping the unwanted upstairs?

And now it's been removed.

As the thudding stops just at the top of the stairs, I struggle to take a breath. Unsure of what's about to come, I glance at Gram. Franticly, she flips through her massive dark red bible, causing pamphlets and little pieces of paper that she used over the years as bookmarks, to fall to the floor. I'm not sure what she hopes to find but I'm willing to try anything at this point.

"I command you in the name of Jesus to go back to where you came." Gram says as the thuds descend the stairs. "I command you in the name of Jesus to go back to where you came! I command you in the name of Jesus to go back to where you came!" She repeats louder and the stairs quiet. Grams eyes meet mine and we both let out a sigh of relief.

I glance over to the doorway where Abigail was standing just moments ago but she's not there anymore. My eyes search the room but there's no sign of her. The curious part of me wonders where she went and if *he* is still on the stairs.

"Emma, I wouldn't go up there if I were you." Gram warns and I realize that I am now standing in the same doorway Abigail was moments ago.

Quietly I continue standing there while I try to listen for any movement upstairs, but there's nothing. Even so, my arms are still covered with goosebumps. Something feels off. I find it hard to believe that Gram chanting that a couple of times scared off this demonic creature. Careful not to bump into anything, I step back to the couch where Gram is. Being a foot away from her, I can hear her battling to breathe. Reaching over, I twist the knob on the oxygen machine and it's so quiet that I can hear the oxygen pulsing through the nasal piece.

Grams hands tremble as she picks up one of her many inhalers. Just as she gets it to her mouth, there is a loud crash, and something tumbles down the stairs. The inhaler drops out of her hand and bounces when it hits the floor.

"I COMMAND YOU IN THE NAME OF JESUS TO GO BACK TO WHERE YOU CAME FROM!" Grams strong and powerful tone surprises me. A door, almost directly above us, slams with such force that the wooden cross hanging on the living room wall falls to the floor. "I... nitro. Nitro, Emma."

Lunging for Grams little denim purse, on the couch next to her, I dig for her nitroglycerin bottle. Why must they make these bottles so small? That alone makes it difficult to find. At the very bottom, under months of mail, receipts, jewelry, and random junk, I find the little brown bottle. In my attempt to shake just one out, more than half the tiny pills fall out and scatter across the floor. Quickly I place one in Gram's hand but she's too weak to grasp it and it falls to the floor with the others. Grabbing another, Gram opens her mouth and I place it under her tongue.

"You'll be okay, Gram. I'm going to call 911." I reach for the phone on the end table next to her, but she covers my hand with hers. The rings on her fingers are loose and keep clashing together from her hands trembling so bad.

"Just. Give. Me. A. Minute." The weakness in her voice breaks my heart. This is all my fault. I need to stop letting everyone's influences change my mind. Simon and Olivia don't have to live here or live with the consequences of stirring up the entities that remain here, I do.

While I give her a minute or so, I run to the kitchen and grab her blood pressure cuff. I need to make myself busy and this information will be helpful when I make the call. Thankfully, Gram doesn't argue about this and lets me wrap the cuff around her small arm. Nonchalantly, I tilt the little screen away from Gram's line of sight. I already know the numbers will be high and if she sees it, she will only stress more. As the monitor beeps, I try even harder not to let the built-up tears stream down my face while I read two hundred over one-forty. This is excessive and not good.

"Try again, Emma." After three more readings just as high as the first, I make the call.

It feels like an hour has passed by the time the ambulance arrives, even though I'm sure it's only been a few minutes. They are always quick to respond when we call. That might have something to do with us living just down the street. I open the front door and the EMT's rush in.

"What's going on Rosalie? I thought Karen just told me you were staying at the nursing home for a little while." By now, we know all of the EMT's, but this woman happens to be one of Aunt Karen's best friends from when they were kids.

"She just got home today." I answer for Gram. "Her blood pressure is high, higher than usual. She's had nitro and I think she needs to be checked out. Something fell down the stairs and she was already worked up before that." I purposely leave out the horrific parts because I know a lot of people don't believe in ghosts. Somethings are simply better left unsaid.

"Thank you, Emma, we will take it from here. Will someone be home soon so you are not left here alone?" Max, the other EMT asks while tightening the straps across Gram on the stretcher.

"My friends are out front, and Grandpa should be back soon. I will let him know what's going on and he should be right behind you guys."

"Are you sure? We didn't see anyone out front." Max and Tina exchange looks.

"They might have gone outback. I'll be fine." Following them outside, I give Gram a kiss on the forehead, and she smiles slightly. "I love you Grammy. I'll be up later." I've rode in the ambulance with her before, but I just feel like I'm in the way. It's also a hard sight to take in as they stabilize her. Seeing the flashing lights disappear down the street while I'm left standing here alone in the driveway is hard enough. Unable to hold back the tears any longer, they stream down my face, and I drop to my knees.

I can't take anymore.

Chapter Eighteen

I finally managed to move to one of Gram's dainty patio chairs on the front porch. It's pitch black by the time anyone comes *home*. I have no idea where Olivia, Esther, Simon, his cousin or Jay went and right now, I could care less. After all, they did leave me here.

Thoughts of setting this house on fire have been running through my mind. I begin contemplating if it would be worth it. *Of course it would,* my subconscious confirms.

"Where is everyone?" David asks, breaking my thoughts.

Keeping my focus on the cars passing by, I say, "Grandpa is at the hospital with Gram. Dad and Jake haven't come back yet. And if you call Olivia, she could probably tell you where her and Esther are."

"Why aren't they here with you?" He sounds irritated, welcome to the club David.

I just shrug my shoulders. "I think the better question is, why am I still here?" Clearly unimpressed with my question, he huffs and continues to walk past me. When the kitchen door closes, I let out a deep breath and slouch down a little.

The kitchen light flickers on, partially lighting up the porch. Thankfully, David leaves the outside light off. Typically, I hate the dark but right now I just want to stay out here in the dark where no one can see me.

I've been out here long enough that the usual obnoxious traffic becomes more like white noise. I can see why Dad and Grandpa spend so much time out here. My eyes feel heavy, and exhaustion sets in like never before. Maybe if I could just clear my head, everything wouldn't be so bad. If only I could get some sleep. After a few deep breaths, I close my eyes and take a few more.

The sun is beaming through the windows, making the white walls and gray floor in the hallway almost cheerful. The birds, directly outside on the powerlines, are chirping and it's the perfect summer morning. I reach the landing at the top of the stairs and as my head turns, I'm quickly reminded that this house could never be cheerful. The red substance continues to ooze down the white wall but it's not so dark now. With the sun hitting it just so, it glistens.

Standing at the beginning of the narrow hallway, leading to the creepy room door, I pause and take a deep breath. What is that smell? Is that gasoline? I glance around me to figure out where it is coming from, but the halls are empty. As empty as they can be.

The creepy room door creaks open, and I take a step backwards and trip over something at my feet. I'm grateful that the old wooden banister is still stable enough to stop me from falling down the stairs. The odor of gasoline gets stronger. Suddenly the birds have stopped chirping and I can hear something dripping.

What in the world? Next to my feet is a red gasoline container that I must have tipped over. The gas is pooling at my feet and beginning to stream down the gaps between the wood planks. Gripping the handle, I stand it back up. What a mess. Why is this even up here?

The door creaks again and my eyes shift up, locking eyes with him. His black eyes peer into mine and I try to look away. The massive black cloak covering him fills the narrow hallway as he stomps towards me. The floor shakes with each step he takes.

Sweat drips off my forehead and I scramble to my feet. The closer he gets, the more difficult it is to breathe. The smell of gasoline fills my senses once more and I know what I have to do.

Trying my damnedest to block him out, I grip the gas container again and walk backwards down the other hall. The gas splashes on the floor as it pours out. I kick the red room door open and hope that he follows me. As horrifying as he is, I'd rather see where he is than not know at all. The door on the other side of the red room is still open and for that, I'm relieved. I don't have any time to waste.

The container is nearly empty by the time I reach the creepy room. I step down into the room and pour what's left and toss the container towards the middle of the room. Reaching into my pants pocket, I pray there is a lighter or matches. The cool metal grazes my finger and I can't help but feel a sense of triumph. This is it. Kneeling in the middle of the creepy room, my thumb swipes down and the small flame appears.

"It's finally over." Just as the container ignites and the peeling wallpaper catches on fire, he lunges towards me, and everything goes dark.

"Emma!" My eyes flutter open and Esther is sitting in a chair next to me. "Why are you outside in the dark all alone?"

My heart is racing, and it takes me a minute to realize where I am. The traffic has started to die down. Aunt Karen's car is the only one in the driveway. Behind me, the gray house still stands, and I feel defeated. *It was just another nightmare.* "My dad and Jake still are not home?"

"They probably won't be home until tomorrow. It's almost midnight though. Where's Grandpa?"

"If you all didn't just leave Gram and I then you would know." I don't have the energy to be angry but I'm also far too exhausted to hide my irritation.

"Well, someone's cranky. Why don't we go to bed?"

Now that I know what needs to be done, I feel more content, not much more but a little. My butt is numb from the patio chair and my neck is kinked but by the time we reach the living room it's not so bad.

"Where are you going Emma? I figured you would want to sleep in the living room after everything thing that happened today." I laugh, fully aware of how crazy I may seem. In my defense, this house could make even the sanest person lose their mind.

"You don't even know the half of it. You didn't see or hear the things that Gram and I did." Hopefully, someone cleaned up the nitroglycerin pills and Baby didn't eat them. She's starting to go blind along with missing half of her teeth, so she eats anything that's small enough for her to just swallow.

"So why are you going up there?" Esther is on my heels as we walk past the couch.

In the hallway at the bottom of the stairs, is one of my bigger porcelain dolls. The head is smashed into thousands of tiny pieces and next to it, lays my teddy bear necklace.

"Did Jake get into your dolls?" I shake my head.

Jake isn't even here and hasn't been since this morning. Why is everyone so quick to blame someone else in this house rather than accepting the actual cause?

"I'm tired of being afraid. If *it* wants me then so be it. I have a plan." I say and push the old button to turn on the hallway light.

"Want me to see if my dad can walk us upstairs?" Her voice cracks and when I turn to face her, there are tears beginning to well up in the corner of her eyes.

"Nope. We will be fine."

Chapter Nineteen

My newfound confidence doesn't help me sleep any better. Esther is still sleeping, and the sun is starting to rise. I press play on the remote for fourth time and Accepted starts playing. I must say, it was a pleasant surprise to find this movie in the DVD player that Esther found at a yard sale yesterday. Neither one of us had heard of it but it has quickly become my favorite movie. I'm still not entirely sure why. Maybe it's because it's a good distraction? It's also funny and what teenage girl doesn't like Justin Long?

During the boring parts, like Schrader's orientation for Harmon College, I weigh out the pros and cons of actually burning this place down. Pros being that we will finally have no choice but to move and no one else will ever have to endure the evil that remains here. Cons being charged with arson. I'm not sure how those charges would go. I've never been in trouble with the police, and I don't keep up with the news like Gram does. Surely, the consequences can't be worse than what I already deal with.

Now for the difficult part. With so many people living here, someone is always in this house. I just have to be patient and wait out for the perfect time. With that being said, I have to be prepared for the perfect time as well. Dad and Grandpa always have a gas container at least half full for the lawn mower and Jakes four-wheeler. The only problem being that it's never put back where they found it. They tend to leave things where they last used them. I guess I will have to keep a closer eye on that.

Luckily, Dad lets me have a lighter for my candles. With the Fourth of July approaching, Tom, one of my older brothers, will be here with sparklers and matches. I'm not sure why, but Tom prefers matches over lighters. That's alright though, especially since this will work in my favor. I need to be as prepared as possible.

Gram will be devastated if she loses everything. Since I have a feeling I have some time before this plan can work, I can start hiding some of her valuables elsewhere. I will have to see if Tom can store them. He loves collecting anything and everything. I'm sure he won't mind. Everything else can be replaced.

Negative thoughts begin to cloud my judgement.

What if the next house we move to is worse? That's not possible. Is it?

What if I can't find Tiggy? He loves to hide, and I wouldn't be able to live with myself if I left him in here. Baby loves to go outside, so she will be easy.

Where would we stay while we found a new place? We might have to separate but I'm sure we could stay with other family members until we can figure it out.

We don't have a lot of money, how are we going to be able to replace clothes and furniture? Gram has shown me her thrifty ways. Between the two of us, we should be able to figure it out.

What about all of the family pictures? There's too many for me to bring them to Tom's without being noticed. I guess we can just hope that they don't burn along with everything else. Although, I can't help but wish the whole place burns completely to the ground. I don't want to leave anywhere for *him* to hide.

"What are you?!" Esther shouts along with Glen, who is holding something that resembles a sea urchin, and I jump.

"Morning."

"Good morning. Did you get some sleep?"

"What is the reasoning for saying good morning? Are you wishing someone a good morning? Or are you insinuating it is a good morning?" That can't be, Esther hasn't been awake long enough to know if it's good or not. "What is a good morning anyways?"

She sighs and drops back on to her pillow. "I take that as a no."

"Correct." Even though I didn't get any sleep at all, I feel refreshed. It was great to finally have some quiet time to let my mind wander and clear a little.

"Does this mean you're going to be cranky like last night?" I'm far from cranky.

"I'm actually in a great mood. So far anyways. We should walk up to the hospital to see Gram. On our way back, we can grab some newspapers and see if any new listing have been added."

"Okay, just let me change. What time is it?"

Digging through the blankets, I finally find my cell phone. "Twelve missed calls? Twenty-three new messages?"

"Olivia tried calling you a few times yesterday. Why didn't you answer?"

"I never heard it ring. I must have left it up here when I went downstairs before everything happened and you all ditched me."

Esther sighs and rolls her eyes. "We didn't mean to. I just thought Gram would be less stressed if we all left for a little while."

"A little while? You didn't come back until what, midnight?"

"I'm sorry Emma. We tried to call you to see if you wanted to stay the night at Olivia's. But when you didn't answer, it was too awkward without you, so I left."

"How did you get home?"

"I walked?"

"By yourself? Are you crazy?" Olivia's house isn't too far but it's still about a mile and a half. So many things could happen in that time. Olivia and I almost got sprayed by a skunk one night walking to her house. Skunks have always scared me. I'd almost rather see a bear.

"Settle down Gram, I'm fine."

The walk to the hospital is peaceful now that I'm finally used to the sound of the traffic. Esther fills me in on what I missed after they all left yesterday. Apparently, they ran into Ring Ding again but this time he had a Banana Twin box on his arm. We both laugh at that potential nickname. Esther is getting nervous about starting at the new school tomorrow. I know she will be fine and make plenty of friends.

Speaking of school, when was the last time I went? Freshman year is almost over, and I can't recall the last full week that I attended. I should probably go tomorrow. I used to love going to school until we moved. Now I just don't have the energy. Gram covers for me though and for that, I'm thankful.

"Emma, will you help me with my hair in the morning?"

"Yeah sure. Just make sure you're up early enough." Maybe this will be the push I need to go.

When we arrive at Gram's room, Grandpa is sitting in the chair next to her. She's sleeping and looks so peaceful. For a brief moment, I consider leaving and coming back later to visit. Gram gets even less sleep than I do.

"Well don't just stand in the doorway. Come over here so I can see you. Charles, hand me my glasses." Gram voice makes

Esther jump. At times, we forget how light of a sleeper Gram is. Grandpa grabs them off the bedside table and helps Gram navigate around the oxygen hose that is looped over her ears.

"How are you feeling, Gram?" She looks so much better than yesterday.

"Better. They think I had another stroke." This makes number four or five now. Gram's been truly fortunate to recover almost one hundred percent after each one.

"I'm sorry. I assume you will be here for a while then." I miss Gram so much when she's not home but it's for the better.

"At least a week and then I will be going back to the nursing home for rehab. Make sure you keep a close eye on Jake. I worry about you all, but he is always getting into something he's not supposed to."

"I am fully aware. I think he stayed with Dad at his girlfriend's last night."

"When you get home, go in and unplug all everything in your fathers' room. Him and Jake love leaving stuff plugged in that doesn't need to be."

"Yes Gram." Although, that may work in my favor. That's an electrical fire just waiting to happen.

"Don't forget to make sure the doors are locked when you go to bed." This is a new concern since we moved to the gray house. Where we used to live, we never had to worry about locking the door. "Check the knobs on that stove too. We don't need the house blowing up. All it takes is one little spark and BOOM!" Gram gestures an explosion with her hands, causing the pulse oximeter to fly off and land in Grandpa's lap. The monitors start beeping and within a blink of an eye, three ladies in scrubs come running in.

"What's going on Rose?" The first one asks and Gram and Grandpa start laughing.

"I'm glad everything's okay. You had us worried for a second." Yeah, they are definitely questioning our sanity. If they only knew.

"Since you're here, you can meet my granddaughter, Emma. She helps me at home."

"Hey." I say awkwardly. Every time Gram is in the hospital, she introduces me to all of her favorite doctors, nurses, housekeepers and anyone else that happens to walk by. Each time is just as awkward, for me anyways. They always seem much more comfortable than I am.

Two hours pass and Gram starts drifting off. Esther and I take that as our cue to leave.

"Alright Grammy, we're going to get going. Get some sleep and I will see you tomorrow."

"Don't forget to check on everything. Maybe you should have wrote it down."

"I've got it. I love you." After a kiss on the tops of our heads we're good to go.

"I see where you get your worrying from. I knew Gram worried but not to that extent." Esther says once we step outside.

I smile.

Thanks to Gram's over worrying, I know exactly how to destroy the gray house.

Chapter Twenty

My alarm starts to go off and after another sleepless night, I wonder why I even bother to set it. The only benefit of not sleeping is that I don't have to worry about the nightmares that come along with it. My day-to-day life is enough of a nightmare. After shutting off the obnoxious alarm, I notice three new messages. I'm terrible at checking my phone and even worse at replying. It's only six, so I guess I can take a few minutes to check them before I have to wake up Esther.

The first one is from Marie.

There is a boy scout dance this weekend. You should go with me! It will be so much fun!

I'm not big on dancing, so I reply with a simple no thank you.

The second and third ones are from Asher.

Would you like a ride to school today?

Sebastian and I are going to the races Friday night. You should come with us. I haven't seen you in a while and I miss you.

Asher's too nice and deserves more. We've been dating on and off since seventh grade, but I just don't know how much longer it will be until he finds someone better that has the time to spend with him. It's not that I don't want to, it's just that I'm already drained. I miss back when things were much simpler. Back when after school meant going to Blockbuster to pick out movies that we never ended up watching. Friday and Saturday nights were spent at the races or the movies. Simple and fun.

That's not the case anymore. Between watching Jake and his creepy little red car, this house and *all* of its tenants, and helping Gram, there's not much of me left. Maybe if I could just get some sleep. *If only.* I laugh and Esther sits up.

"What's so funny?"

"Nothing." I get up and plug in my hair straightener. "Ready when you are."

"Please don't burn me." Esther begs as she slowly sits on the black metal stool in front of me.

"I'll try not to. I have been straightening mine for a few years now. You'll be fine." Just as I squeeze the flat iron together, she turns her head, pulling her light brown hair out of my grasp. "Stay still or one of us is going to get burned." I warn.

"Sorry. We should walk to school today! I'll have to walk a little way by myself since the high school is closer, but it would be fun."

"I'm not sure if I'm going today. I didn't sleep again and I kind of just want to go see Gram." That will also leave plenty of time to gather some of Gram's valuables. Which will make tomorrow the perfect day to finally put an end to everything. Aunt Karen and Dad will be at work. Grandpa will be at the hospital visiting Gram. Esther and Jake will be at school. So that just leaves David.

"Oh please. Emma, you never sleep! You can't use that as an excuse with me anymore. Also, we can go see Gram after school."

"Why don't you ask your dad. If he says yes, then I will walk with you."

"Okay!"

Twenty minutes later, Esther is satisfied with her hair. I grab my clothes and take a quick shower. Back in my room, I pick up my black eyeliner pencil and am shocked at my reflection. The dark circles around my eyes are bolder than usual and my eyes are bloodshot. I need some sleep, and soon. My cover up doesn't do much but it's better than nothing. After quickly straightening my hair, I feel a little better. I'm still undecided about school though. I know I *should* go.

As I make my way downstairs, I glance down the narrow hallway. The creepy room door is still closed, and it was unexpectedly quiet up here last night. It's not over though, I can feel it. It's more like the calm before the storm. A storm I hope I'm not too exhausted to get through.

"Dad, can I walk to school with Emma today?"

"No. I need to make sure that you actually go." David glares at me as I walk in the kitchen, and I roll my eyes. "Grab your backpack and I will drive you and Jake to school."

"I'll walk." I say, full of sarcasm.

"Why? The kid with the shoes is waiting in the driveway for you." David has some odd fascination with Asher's shoes, and I have no idea why.

Crap. I never texted him back. This is what I mean, I'm terrible at replying. I swing my school bag over my shoulder and run outside. Sure enough, Asher's little silver car is in the middle of the driveway.

"Hey! You didn't reply so I figured I would just stop by and see if you wanted a ride." He smiles as I open the passenger door and I find it hard to tell him that I'm not going to school today. Or at least, I wasn't until now.

"I'm sorry. I wasn't sure if I was going or not. My Gram's back in the hospital and I'm just exhausted."

He laughs and pushes his dark brown hair off to one side of his forehead. "That's because it's Monday." I wish that were the reason. "How's she doing?" It's sweet of him to ask about her, even though he doesn't call the house phone unless he absolutely needs too. About a year ago he called, and she went up one side of him and down the other. She may scare him but he's too nice to dismiss her wellbeing.

My eyes drift up towards the window above the front porch and there she is. Abigail is standing in the window with the most heart breaking look on her face. "Do you see someone in that window?" I blurt, and instantly I regret asking because I'm sure he doesn't see her. Aside from Gram and I, no one seems to see her. It's starting to become frustrating.

He looks up and shakes his head, causing his hair to cover his eyes again. "That's the scary room or whatever right?" He's one of the few people that have no interest in seeing that room. And for that, I'm appreciative.

"Yeah, it is." My head starts pounding and I massage my temples. These headaches are getting worse every day. Gram and Aunt Karen get them frequently too. I wonder is this is part of our *gift*. Wait, he just asked a question before I rudely changed the subject. What was it? Oh yeah, Gram. "Um... she seemed good yesterday but I'm not sure. I was going to visit her today, but I'll go later."

"Maybe after you see her, we could hang out?" He's playing with his lip ring waiting patiently for my answer.

It would be fun. "I'll see if Karen and David are cooking tonight. If not, I will have to." His smile starts to fade so quickly I add, "I'll let you know." Sometimes I wish that I could be a regular teenager, instead of having so many responsibilities and worries.

The ride to school doesn't take long and I find myself wishing school was a little further away. Asher is going on about all the work he wants to do to his car and even though I have little to no idea what most of it means, it's nice to finally have some normalcy. I need more of this.

As Asher parks in front of the school, I start to feel anxious. I already know that I'm going to end up spending most of the day discussing make up work with all of my teachers. I still have the last stack of assignments in my bag that I have to hand in.

"Welcome back." Asher says and I take a deep breath and smile. This is it. From here on out, I am going to start being more like an average teenager.

"Thanks." I can do this. Going to school is a part of being a normal teenager. The time away from that house is much needed. Already, my head feels a little clearer. I need this. Before I can forget, I send Aunt Karen a message about dinner. I'm sure it will be a while before she has a chance to reply but it's still early enough.

His arm drapes over my shoulder while we wait for an opportunity to cross the parking lot. I forgot how nice he smells and how comforting being near him feels. "Did you get my message about the races?"

"I did and I'd like to go!" I answer quickly before I can overthink it and change my mind.

Chapter Twenty-One

Before I know it, the school day is almost over. Just like I anticipated, most of it was spent exchanging make-up assignments. Aunt Karen still hasn't messaged me back about dinner and I decide not to worry about it today. Today has been the perfect day and I'm not ready to step back to reality just yet. After History class Asher is waiting for me in the hallway. I'm not sure how he does it, but he always seems to be waiting for me outside of each class. Even when I'm not spending five to ten minutes catching up with the teachers.

"Have you heard from your aunt?" He asks as his fingers intertwine with mine, creating butterflies in my stomach; that's something I haven't felt in a long time.

"No, but they can figure it out." I'm not ready to go back. I'm still surprised that today has been the best day I've had in far too long. I'll keep that to myself though. Some may think that's awfully pathetic considering it was spent at school. "So, what are we doing now?"

"Well, I can bring you back to your house or to the hospital."

I shake my head. "I was thinking we could hang out instead. Unless you have other plans." If he does, that's fine. I certainly don't expect him to drop everything for me. But at the same time, I can't help but hope that he doesn't have any plans.

"Oh, okay! I haven't seen or heard from Sebastian today so besides homework, I don't have any plans." I expect him to ask why the change of plans, but he doesn't. Instead, he grins and reaches for my bag while we wait for a break in the traffic so we can cross the road.

"Have you gotten taller?" Maybe it's because we haven't spent much time together but standing here next to him makes me feel shorter than usual. He must be almost a foot taller than me now. Dad tells me that I'll be lucky if I get any taller which is fine.

He chuckles and shrugs his shoulders. "I don't know, maybe. Or maybe you're just shrinking." Opening the passenger door, his fingers release mine and the usual sadness sinks in. As if he realizes this, he wraps his arms around me tightly, squeezing out the sadness.

I needed this.

The ride to his house takes me back. Back to the simple and carefree days. The windows are down, blowing my hair in front of my face and I regret not keeping a hair tie or clip in my school bag. Some Offspring song is playing, and he insists that it will sound better once he replaces the stereo. I think it sounds fine, but I guess I don't have anything to compare it to.

I must say, he's getting better at driving a standard. With each stop, he still takes a deep breath before taking off and I pretend not to notice. It's pretty cute though. I've missed him more than I knew.

"Is your Gram going to be mad that you're not going up to see her today?"

"I don't think so. I'll call her later." If anything, she will probably be glad that I'm getting out of the house. He may think that she doesn't like him, but she does. We all joke that if Gram yells at you or gives you crap, it's because she truly cares about you. There are a few exceptions to that, but Asher is not one of them.

I never thought the sight of the huge white house with the wrap around porch would be so comforting. His house has to have twice as many windows as the gray house but it's not creepy in the least bit. I know I can glance up at any window and there will not be any apparitions staring back. There is, however, a couple of extremely excited dogs. We barely make it to the bottom step on the porch and we can hear the dogs running towards the door. I can't help but laugh when they practically take the both of us out when Asher opens the door to toss his backpack inside.

"I think they missed you. Come sit with me." Asher reaches for my hand and pats the empty cushion next to him on the wicker couch beside me on the porch.

I'm hesitant about sitting. For the first time in over a year, I don't feel completely exhausted, and I have a feeling it's only a matter of time before it catches up to me.

"Is something wrong?"

"No, it's just... I don't want to fall asleep."

He laughs and pulls my arm until I'm standing in front of him. "I'm not that boring, am I?"

"No! That's not it." I laugh. It feels good, I can't remember the last time before today where I genuinely laughed. "I hardly sleep anymore, and I remember all too well how comfortable this couch is."

"I'll keep you awake." He winks, reminding me of the flirt that he always has been.

"No necking." I jokingly remind him, and we both start laughing.

After hours of catching up, pushing boundaries, and multiple warnings from Asher's mom about keeping it PG, the sun starts to set. Dread takes over because that means it's time to go back to the gray house. Today went by too fast and my stomach literally hurts from laughing so hard. Slowly we make our way across the driveway to Asher's car. I get the feeling he isn't ready to go either. Offspring picks up where it left off. It's not lost on me that he's going five under the speed limit the whole way. I was right, neither one of us are ready for today to end.

The summer night air feels wonderful. I close my eyes and let my head rest against the back of the seat. "Thank you for today."

"Anytime." Between shifting gears, his hand rests on my thigh. "Would you like a ride to school tomorrow?"

"Yes please." I know it's unrealistic for everyday to be as great as today but I'm not about to pass up any possible chance at being just a regular teenage girl. Even if it's just for a short moment.

Grandpa, Dad and David are waiting on the front porch when we pull into the driveway. Before they can make their way over to the car, our lips part and I quickly get out in hopes to save any embarrassment from The Three Stooges.

"Hey, where's my kiss?" Davis shouts to Asher before he backs out of the driveway.

Asher puckers his lips and yells back, "Come over here."

Chapter Twenty-Two

Dad sighs and drops his hands to his sides. "Asher's leaving so soon? I had a question for him. One of the carpenters at the job site today said he has a car just like his. He's looking to part out. I was going to see if there was anything in particular that he was looking for."

"Sorry Dad, I think David scared him off. I can let him know though."

"I just wanted a kiss too!" David whines and out of the corner of my eye, I can see Grandpa shaking his head.

"Well don't forget. I'm not sure how long he will have it and he's even going to throw in some tires."

Before I can assure Dad that I won't forget, Esther whips the kitchen door open.

"And just where have you been today, missy?"

"School?"

"Obviously. I mean after school?" Not much goes unsaid in this house, so I know she already knows where I was.

"Your grandmother wants you to call her." Grandpa interrupts, moving his cigar to the corner of his mouth.

"I'll call her now, Grandpa."

In the kitchen, something smells like Thanksgiving dinner and the table is cluttered with dinner dishes. I guess they managed simply fine without me. Before brushing my teeth, I check on the stove to make sure all of the knobs are in the off position. I already know that's going to be on Gram's checklist for today.

Dragon Ball Z is blaring from the living room T.V and somehow Jake is sleeping through it. Stepping over him and his blankie, I turn the volume down. I know if I shut it off, he will wake up. At least when he's sleeping, I don't have to worry as much about his whereabouts or what he's doing.

At the bottom of the stairs, Esther is so close that she steps on the back of my flipflop. Normally, this would irritate me but not today. I've had a great day and I'm going to try my best to keep the momentum going. Besides, it's pretty much bedtime... for Esther anyways.

As I press the button for the upstairs hallway light, I close my eyes and take a deep breath. *Stay calm and don't let them bother you.* I repeat with each step.

Just as my eyes are level with the floor ahead of us, I can see the rusty old chains in the doorway to the little pink room. I inhale sharply and cover my mouth. *Stay calm and don't let them bother you.* Deliberately, I avoid looking in that direction as we get closer. Maybe if I just ignore them, they will leave me alone.

That seems to work, as I don't hear the chains clink together when we pass by.

The creepy room door is cracked open, and I try not to hurry past. *Stay calm and don't let them bother you.*

At last, we reach my room. Since Esther is the last one, she pushes the door to close it. In the gap, between the door and the casing, there are glowing eyes glaring at me. I gasp and jump backwards. I try to look away, but I can't.

Esther slams the door the rest of the way closed and whips around. "What is it, Emma?"

"Nothing. I just um… tripped." I lie. There's no point for me to explain to her about what I just saw. And I know *they* can hear us. I don't want to feed into it. Not tonight.

"Yeah okay." She says derisively.

I raise my index finger to my lips. "Shh."

Taking this as her opening to change the subject, she asks the question that I know she has been dying to know the answer to. "So, are you going to tell me about your afternoon?" Her eyebrows wiggle and we both chuckle.

"I have to call Gram." I answer and dig through my bag for my phone.

"Oh, come on. Don't leave me hanging!"

Just like I assumed, Gram is not mad that I didn't visit her today. In fact, she is thrilled to hear that I had a great day at school and got to spend time away from the house after. She continues to express how much better Asher is compared to some boyfriend that Aunt Karen had when she was younger. This isn't the first time she has told me the story, but I just patiently listen and let her finish. After reassuring her that I already checked the stove, she wishes me a good night and hangs up. I find myself a little amazed that there is no list of concerns tonight.

By the time I am done talking to Gram, Esther is sleeping. Why can't I fall asleep that easy?

Since I do not feel tired, I decide to start catching up on my school assignments. Just as I start laying my books around me on the floor, Tiggy curls up in my lap. He used to make himself comfortable on whichever book I needed. After moving him every time, I think he is finally realizing that he was in the way. I can't imagine sleeping on books is very comfortable anyways.

By the time I'm done with Algebra it's only ten and Tiggy is sound asleep in my lap. I have always found it comforting watching him sleep. He wakes up for almost any sound, ready to check it out and attack if necessary. So, when he's sleeping, things just feel safe and content.

English is going to be the most time consuming since I still have to read all of The Great Gatsby. If I want to be able to stay focused on it, I should probably start reading it now. Jake and Esther are sleeping so there are minimal distractions. Reaching up behind me, I pull a pillow and my fuzzy blanket off my bed. Tiggy lifts his head and peeks around with one eye open before relaxing again. I cover the both of us up and begin reading.

"And so, with the sunshine and the great bursts of leaves growing on the trees, just as things grow in fast movies, I had that familiar conviction that life was beginning over again with the summer."

I read Nick Carraway's thoughts over and over. Maybe this too, could be true for me. Today still feels implausible. Almost like I had imagined it. But I can't stop myself from wondering if this could possibly be a new beginning.

Maybe I don't have to live in fear anymore. With summer vacation quickly approaching, there will be more things to do, and I won't be in this house as much. I could probably find some babysitting jobs. That would not only get me out of this house, but I would also be able to start saving some money. Money, that's the solution to getting the hell out of this house.

Jazz music fills my ears. My eyes dart around the room, it's crowded with people. The floral wallpaper begins to feel as if it's closing in on us. I need some fresh air. Making my way through the small but crowded room is more challenging than I expected. I glance around, hoping to find a familiar face. Everything looks different. Short dresses are covered with frill. Thick headbands are worn by nearly every woman. Feathers are floating in the heavy air.

"Where am I?" I mutter under my breath.

"Welcome to the party!" A deep voice comes from behind me.

I can't bring myself to turn around. Something about that voice sounds familiar and not in a good way. Fear and panic set in, there's no way I'm looking now. Instead, I hurry towards the door. Trying to squeeze through the doorway is impossible as people continue to flood in. Two people push against me, and I'm stuck. I've never felt this claustrophobic.

"Excuse me! I need to get through!" I shout but no one seems to hear me over the excessively loud band.

"Follow me." The deep voice is inches away from my ear, causing chills to run down my spine.

Just as someone's hand touches my shoulder, I switch to full panic mode.

"STOP TOUCHING ME!" I whip around and there are those eyes, glowing and glaring into mine. My breath catches and everything goes dark.

"Emma! Shh, it's just a nightmare. Emma, look at me!" My eyes open wide, and Esther is kneeling a couple of feet in front of me. "Are you okay?" Tears stream down her face and within seconds I can feel my own tears, mixed with sweat, dripping down my face.

I nod. It was just a nightmare; I realize when I look down at The Great Gatsby on top of the fuzzy blanket. Damn Fitzgerald.

Chapter Twenty-Three

It takes almost an hour to convince Esther that I'm okay. It's almost two by the time she falls back asleep. Now that I am fully awake, I pick up The Great Gatsby and continue reading.

Glowing eyes fill my thoughts. After a few minutes of trying my hardest to stay focused, I can't do it any longer. I slide a little crumpled piece of paper in between the pages as a bookmark and return it to the stack of assignments.

Maybe a movie will help. Knowing that Accepted is still in the DVD player, I press play. Esther groans as she pulls her blanket over her face and rolls over. I'm sure she's ready to have her own room. I'm not sure if I am though. As much as I don't want to admit, I enjoy sharing a room with her.

Tiggy cuddles up next to me when I sit back down on the floor. A cold chill runs through me just as my fingertips graze my history textbook. That's odd. Tiggy's ears are drawn back but his eyes are closed. What's he listening to? Trying to shake off the unnerving sense, I pick up the health book instead.

• • •

My eyes begin to feel heavy after several assignments are completed, I feel like I'm making great progress on catching up. At this rate I should be caught up by Friday. Refusing to fall asleep, I stand and pace. Dad and Jake are asleep in the room below me, so I'm extra cautious to keep my steps light.

Tiggy's eyes pop open and he's quick on his paws. I partly expect him to start clawing at the door, but he jumps up in front of the T.V instead.

"What's wrong Tiggy?"

Without acknowledging me, he stares intently at the screen. Of course, this catches my attention and I too, stand there in anticipation. Go figure that it's at the only scary part of the movie. Luckily for me, I've seen it more than enough times. So, I already know what's going to happen.

"Okay guys seriously, I don't want to be here when the walls start to bleed." I totally understand your fears, Schrader! Just be thankful they don't. I still do not understand why Bartleby tried putting the ceiling back in place. Obviously, the broken tile is not going to stay put without anything securing it. Whatever, it's just a movie.

Tiggy scrunches his face and starts growling.

"It's alright, dude. We already know a skeleton falls from the ceiling." Is that what he's so on edge about? I laugh and grab the remote to fast forward, but it drops onto the floor. Tiggy hisses and just as I look back up at the screen, I'm breathless. The two glowing eyes from when we first came up here last night and from my nightmare are across the middle of the screen, one is bloodshot. I gasp and cover my mouth. *I cannot let them see that I'm frightened.*

Scrambling to pick up the remote, I click the power button as soon as I feel it under my thumb. Only the T.V doesn't respond. Frantically, I press the little red button again and again. Nothing happens. The eyes are still there, burning further into my memory.

Tiggy lets out what almost sounds like a squeal, and I rip the power cord for the T.V out of the power strip. The eyes linger until gradually fading away.

"What the hell just happened?" I've watched that movie numerous times and I know that is *not* part of it. Nervously, I scan the room. Everything looks fine.

Breathe. I need to breathe.

After my breathing returns back to normal, I turn on my stereo. I've come to learn that it's not so bad up here if I have background noise on. Maybe I will not be getting caught up as quickly as I thought.

Yet again, the annoying alarm on my phone sounds. I'm not sure if the tune itself is annoying, or if I'm more so annoyed by the fact that I can't sleep. Either way, I shut it off and gather all of my textbooks and assignments to put back into my school bag.

"What time is it?" Esther groans and peeks over the blankets.

"Six. Did you want me to do your hair today?"

"No, I'm too tired. Wake me up at seven." *Too tired?* She doesn't even know what it's like to be tired.

"Okay." Tiggy starts clawing at the door, I'm sure he's ready for breakfast. I could use a shower to give me some energy. Deciding on a pair of jeans, a tank top and a hoodie, I open the door and Tiggy bolts halfway down the hall before jumping through the railing, missing half the staircase. Too bad I couldn't do that.

Straight ahead, through the red room doorway, the elderly lady is sitting in her wheelchair looking out the window. Since she never bothers me, I try to return the favor by tip toeing down the hall. My luck falls short as I reach the other end of the hallway.

"Ignoring us won't do you any good." A deep whisper reverberates in my ear. I recognize this voice, but where have I heard it?

Before I can turn around, something pushes against my back. I reach for the railing but there's nothing close enough to grab and before I know it, I'm lying on the floor at the bottom of the stairs.

Glowing eyes peer down at me, paralyzing me. "Get out!" He screams.

Within seconds Esther is running down the stairs. "Oh, my goodness, Emma! Are you alright?"

I try to tell her no, but I can't. I try to look up at her, but my eyes are too focused on the glowing ones peering into mine.

"What just happened?" Dad and Jake are standing in their bedroom doorway.

Jake looks down at the little red car in his hand and shakes his head. "No. Bad friend!" He scolds.

"What the hell is going on?" Grandpa hurries from the kitchen. "You kids need to be careful on these stairs."

"This house is literally going to kill me!" I try to scream but the words hardly come out as a whisper.

Grandpa chuckles and helps Esther pull me up off the floor. "Jesum crow, there is nothing wrong with this house! Would you let it go already?"

Let it go? What else has to happen for someone to listen to me? Why am I the only one it seems to detest? I hate this house more and more with each day that drags by. Slowly, I'm beginning to resent everyone that lives here too.

By the time I make it to the kitchen, I have officially woken up everyone in the house. Aunt Karen and David are just standing there as I stomp past. Any other morning, I would check to see if anyone needed to use the only bathroom this house has before I take a shower. Not today though. They can all wait.

Chapter Twenty-Four

When the hot water turns cold, I decide it's finally time to get out of the shower. I hope no one else wanted a warm shower. Actually, I hope they did. I hope all of them did. I'm fed up with no one listening to me.

"Emma! Hurry up! I need to use the bathroom!" Aunt Karen shouts and knocks on the door. "I hope you didn't use all the hot water!" She adds.

"You're going to make us all late!" David complains before knocking as well. Other than dropping Esther and Jake off at school, he doesn't really have anywhere that he needs to be. So, I don't really understand what his problem is.

After taking my time getting dressed, I unlock the door and try not to laugh at the sighs of frustration and relief coming from the other side. How does it feel being ignored?

"Next time, why don't you see if anyone needs to use the bathroom before you spend an hour in there." Aunt Karen and David say louder than necessary as I push past them.

If this were any other day, I would probably continue past them, but I've had enough. I've had enough of this house. I've had enough of everyone that lives here. With the exception of Esther. I've had enough of being tortured by spirits. I'm done.

I spin around, a little too fast and for a few seconds the room spins. "If you guys have such a problem with it then why don't you start looking for a bigger place? With more than one bathroom!" I yell and stomp through the kitchen. Someone mutters something but I know if I go back, I will say something I will regret.

"Obviously, she's pissed off!" Esther yells loud enough that I can hear her once I reach the bottom of the stairs. "And I don't blame her! None of you see the horrible things she does! None of you lose sleep or have nightmares like Emma does! So, unless you are going to try and better this whole situation, then stop complaining!"

Wait. What just happened? Did someone really just take my side? Footsteps are coming towards me but I'm too shocked to move.

"What?" Esther asks and cautiously walks around me to go up the stairs.

"What the hell was that about?" I snap, not meaning to.

Pausing halfway up, she turns to face me. "Nothing. I was just sticking up for you. You're welcome by the way."

"Oh. Thank you. I'm sorry I didn't leave you any hot water." I follow behind, ignoring the paranormal audience surrounding us. The guy with the eyes has his head tilted down but that doesn't stop him from glaring at us. A cool breeze passes by, and Abigail appears at the end of the hallway by my bedroom door.

"Leave them alone!" Abigail hisses.

I glance up at Esther, trying to see if she sees what's going on, but she just continues towards our room. I still can't fathom that Esther doesn't see what I see. What if she's just pretending? Maybe she does see them.

She surprises me by chuckling. "Oh, don't be! I took a shower last night."

I smile and give her a light hug, clearly stunning both of us.

"Um... Emma?" Esther begins.

"Yeah?" When she doesn't respond, I toss my eyeliner pencil down and look over at her. She's pointing out the window and out of nowhere, something black falls outside my window. "What was that?"

"I was hoping you would know!"

"Just fly! Flap your wings!" Jake's voice echoes through my room as I slide the window open. "I already showed you how!"

Peeking down from the window, Jake is standing there holding a pigeon. I drop the window, swipe up my school bag and run downstairs. How the hell did he catch a pigeon?

"Jake! What are you doing? Those birds could make you sick!"

"Emma, I just want to help it fly!" He argues and tosses the poor bird up as high as he can, which has to be over ten feet. I'm impressed. The poor bird isn't impressed and doesn't even try to flap its wings. It just nose dives onto the grass and tumbles around until Jake runs over and picks it up. "Why don't you want to fly? I would like to fly!"

"I think it has had enough practice for now, Jake. You need to go wash your hands. It's time to go to school."

"But. But! Birdie is so close to flying!"

"I think you mean close to dying..."

Jake squeezes the pigeon against his chest and whips around to face me. "Don't say that! I love Birdie!"

"Come on Esther and Jake!" David interrupts and for once, I'm glad. I'm still irritated with him and Aunt Karen but at least Birdie can get a rest.

Jake runs out back and I chase after him to make sure he doesn't bring Birdie inside. That's the last thing we need. He stops in front of a medium sized dog crate, that I've never seen before, and gently places Birdie inside before securing the door.

"Where did you get a dog crate? How long has this been out here?" I pause before asking my next question. I'm not entirely sure I want to know the answer. "Just how many flying lessons have you put Birdie through?"

"David found it." He shrugs his little shoulders. "I found Birdie after school."

He runs up the stairs and slams the kitchen door before clarifying which day after school. Since it's Tuesday, I can only hope it was yesterday and not Friday.

Maybe Grandpa hasn't left yet, and he can take care of Birdie before Jake gets out of school. I know Jake will be devastated when he gets home and Birdie is gone, but this isn't healthy for either one of them.

Back out front, Grandpa is talking to Asher, who is grinning, and I begin to wonder what they could possibly be talking about. My attention is stolen when I see David is pulling out of the driveway while Jake is waving out the back window. Perfect.

"Hey!" Asher is still grinning, and I can't help but do the same. "Your Grandpa was just telling me that your dad came across a car that I might be interested in."

"Hey! Oh, yeah. You can ask him about it later. He didn't tell me much about it. It comes with tires, that's all I know." He pulls me in for a hug, memories of yesterday afternoon transpire, and I've never felt more ready for school. More so after school but the school day yesterday actually went well.

Grandpa starts to head back to the house, and I almost forgot about Birdie. "Wait! Grandpa, did you know that Jake has been trying to teach a pigeon to fly?" Grandpa and Asher tilt their heads before snickering. "Seriously! He even has it in a cage out back. He said David found it for him."

"Jesum crow. Aright, you kids have a good day at school. I'll go take care of it." Grandpa's shoulders slouch as a puff of cigar smoke clouds between us.

"Thank you, Grandpa."

Asher is still laughing when I get in and buckle. "I knew I should have got here a little early today."

"Why is that?"

"I wish I could have seen the flying lessons."

I smile and shake my head. Maybe today won't be as bad as it started.

Chapter Twenty-Five

Once again, the school day passes by quickly. Mr. Jones was impressed that I was able to complete all of my assignments for Algebra in one night. Maybe tonight I can get through the rest of my English assignments. Probably not. I have a feeling that tonight will be anything but quiet.

In the hall, Asher is leaning against a locker waiting for me. He has definitely grown taller. He was *not* taller than the lockers a couple of months ago.

We still haven't discussed today's plans. We were too occupied by Jake's flying lessons this morning. Hopefully Grandpa took care of Birdie after we left.

"Well, you look happier than this morning!" Asher smiles and slides his arm around my back. It's a sweet gesture but it's slightly awkward to walk without tripping. I'm not about to mention it though.

"That's because I am." Two days in a row, I have been able to spend time with him. My grade is high enough to pass Algebra now, that's one less class that I will have to retake next year. I'm not at the house. I get a break from watching Jake. I know Gram is in good hands. For the first time in a long time, I actually have a reason to feel happy. Well, *reasons*.

"Do you have to be home right after school?"

The gray house is not my home. I want to say, but I decide not to. "Nope. Not today. Do you have any plans?" If I don't have to go back to that house anytime soon, I'll be even happier.

"My mom wants me to mow the lawn, but I can do that later. Wanna hang out at my house again?" I guess I'm not the only one in a good mood today. Asher is almost always in a good mood but something's different today.

"Your mom won't mind?" I know in the past she was concerned that we were spending too much time together, and I felt bad after for not realizing we were.

"Nah." He shakes his head and smiles. "We can go pick out a couple of movies or study. What would you like to do?"

I'll have more than enough time for homework later. A Blockbuster marathon is just what I need. "Alright, let's pick out some movies!"

The familiar scent of Blockbuster fills my senses and I feel lighter. The stress of my not-so-typical-life begins to dissolve with each step and laugh. Since we already know that we most likely won't be watching them, we pick two movies that Asher's mom will enjoy. I didn't realize just how long it has been since we have been here, until I glance around and no longer recognize the movies surrounding us. In the past we sometimes had to rent ones that we already rented because we had made our way through all of the new releases. I guess we have some catching up to do.

Offspring has been swapped for Fall Out Boy for the ride to his house. Either one is fine with me, but the change is nice, I suppose. Once again, we are welcomed by a couple of overly excited dogs when Asher opens the front door. In the living room, I make myself comfortable and curl up on the couch while he starts the movie and grabs us something to drink.

"Emma, did you want..." He starts and I open my eyes. "Oh, I'm sorry. I didn't mean to wake you up. I take it you weren't able to get much sleep last night either?"

Much sleep? Try none. At all. Except for those few minutes. I shake my head. "It's okay." Scooting up a little, I swing my feet off the comfy couch onto the floor. Maybe this will help me stay awake. That's wishful thinking.

Between the comfortable couch, his arm around me while my head rests against his chest, the slow beat of his heart, and the familiar scent of laundry soap mixed with his cologne, I feel myself drifting off again.

Blackness surrounds me, suffocating me. I try to back away, but I'm cornered. The stomping of footsteps get closer and closer.

Boom.

Boom.

BOOM.

"Hey! Emma, are you okay?" Asher's panicked voice breaks through my nightmare.

My heart is racing, and I jump off the couch as quick as I can. My hands are trembling when I look down and I shake them, in hopes to get them to stop. That does nothing. I can't breathe. I need some space. Something makes a loud thud on the other side of the wall behind the couch, and I can't stop the shriek that escapes me. Asher stands and pulls me against his chest. I try to push him away, but he tightens his grip.

"I... I. I have to go." I blurt and twist so that he has to loosen his grip. At last, I'm free and I don't stop running until I'm outside.

"Wait, that was just the bunnies on the stairs!" He shouts, his voice following behind me.

Finally, I can take a deep breath once I reach the grass. The warm summer night air has never felt so refreshing.

"What's going on Emma? I've never seen you so scared. Is *that* why you're not sleeping?" Of course, that's why I'm not sleeping. If anyone even knew about just half of what my nightmares consist of, they wouldn't sleep either. He reaches for me, and I take a step back. The confliction is clear in his eyes, but I know if I even try to explain, he's going to think I'm crazy. Not even my family believes me.

"I'm sorry. I have to go." I confess.

"Just tell me what's going on, please?" He reaches for my hand, but I take a few more steps back. I can't handle anyone being close to me right now. "I can close the door, so the bunnies stay off the stairs." His eyes fall to the space between us. "Please don't leave upset like this."

I can see the hurt in his eyes, and it breaks my heart, but I can't do this right now. Right now, I just need to scream before my head bursts. Which means I need to go.

I turn towards the sidewalk, and he touches my arm. I stop and take a deep breath. *Don't freak out. Don't freak out.*

"At least let me give you a ride home." He whispers and I relax a little.

"Thank you, Asher. I appreciate it but I'm going to walk. I need some space to clear my head." Even though no amount of space or alone time is going to do a damn thing to rid my nightmares, find a new place to live, or eliminate the level of frustration and hatred I have towards everyone that lives in the gray house.

He sighs and looks up at me one last time with sadness in his eyes. "I love you."

Chapter Twenty-Six

What?

I mean, yeah, we have said "I love you" to each other before, but this feels different. More intimate. More sincere. More real. More mature. And right now, after all of that, he decides to drop this on me? No, this cannot be happening right now.

"Emma, say something." Asher reaches for my hand and laces his fingers between mine. The usual relaxation that comes along with his touch has been replaced with insecurity and hesitation.

I'm almost sixteen. My thoughts should be boys, and make-up, and gossip or whatever average sixteen-year-old girls fret over. Not taking care of my little brother. Not being a live-in nurse to my grandmother who has two of her own children living at home temporarily. Not worrying about whether or not today will be the day the gray house swallows me whole. Bullshit. This is all completely bullshit. I should be crying over the fact that my boyfriend just sincerely told me he loves me, not because of how messed up my life is. I should be running into his arms, not stepping away from him.

My thoughts are colliding with each other, causing my head to pound. I begin to open my mouth, but nothing comes out. I'm frozen.

"Come on, please let me give you a ride home. Your bag is still in my car anyways."

Home. I resent that word. The gray house could never be anyone's home. Yeah, I keep my stuff there but even that's questionable and most certainly doesn't make it my home. Home is somewhere you feel safe and comfortable. Somewhere you can go to escape the world. Home is somewhere that you can sleep peacefully and let your worries go away. That is not the gray house. That will never be the gray house.

Before my brain can comprehend my actions, I tug my hand away, turn towards the sidewalk and run. I run as fast as I can until I'm gasping for air and sweat is dripping down my forehead. I feel like a fish out of water.

I can't juggle everything anymore. Something has got to give. How could I have been so naive to think for even a second that I could?

I can't. It is just not possible.

Suddenly, my legs give out from exhaustion, and I drop. The concrete is unforgiving, and I can already feel my knees bruising. It takes all I have left to push myself away from the road and closer to the stone wall. The wall is cool against my back as I pull my knees to my chest and focus on regulating my breathing.

Something warm and wet touches the palms of my hands. Under the flickering streetlight, I can see blood soaking through my jeans. The already worn-out material is now ripped across my right knee and there is a decent size gash that more blood is flowing from.

"Why am I bleeding?" My eyes scan the area where I fell and something glimmers. Leaning forward, I can now see the broken beer bottle.

Awesome. So much for another day as a regular teenager.

Could this day get any worse? Probably, since I more than likely just jinxed myself.

What am I going to do? Even if I wanted to, I don't trust myself to walk all the way to the gray house. *You should have accepted Asher's offer for a ride home*, my subconscious reminds me, but I push her away. Olivia's house is about five minutes from here, but if I show up bleeding her mom is going to have so many questions, because she actually cares about her kids and their friend's wellbeing. I don't have the energy for that.

Annoyed, I pull myself up and lean against the stone wall. "Think. There must be somewhere else to go or someone to call." I reach into the pockets of my jeans, but they are empty. "Dammit!" My phone is still in my school bag, which is still in Asher's car.

Oh, I know. Tom! My brother Tom only lives down the hill.

With each step the pain in my knees worsen and I can feel the legs of my pants sticking further down. I kind of wish that I would have worn sneakers. They would have been stained with blood but at least I would not be leaving so much of a trail, like my flipflops are.

Thankfully, I can see the apartment complex where Tom lives with our mother. I take a deep breath and force my legs to move a little faster.

"I can do this." Just a little further.

Relief washes over me when I finally reach their apartment door. My knuckles bang against the door softer than I intended, I'm not sure if anyone even heard me. I raise my fist to knock again but the blinds covering the window move before the door opens.

Tom's jaw drops and he jumps to the side so I can walk past him. I cringe at the mess I'm leaving behind. Hopefully Mom isn't here, and I have some time to get it cleaned up. At least the flooring is tile and not carpet.

"Stay here." Tom orders as he runs upstairs.

Please grab the first aid kit and not Mom. I hear the hallway closet door close before he runs back down holding out the first aid kit. "Thank you!"

"What happened to you? Should we call the police?" The panic in his voice is clear. Tom worries just as much as I do, to the point that people are shocked that we don't share the same grandmother.

"Thank you, Tom. I just fell, there's no need to call the police. Is Mom here?" My voice is weak while I pull up my blood-soaked pant leg. Blood is everywhere from the bottom of my thigh, over my knee and down my leg. My foot is hardly noticeable and my flipflop is stuck to my foot.

Yep, definitely jinxed myself.

His eyes are wide and stay locked on my knee. "You fell? From where and onto what?"

"I was running and fell onto a glass bottle. Do you have a towel or something so that I don't make more of a mess? It's bad enough that the entryway looks like a crime scene."

"Oh, um yeah, hang on." He tosses me one of the decorative kitchen towels hanging from the handle on the oven door, and I shake my head. I don't have to live here to know that those towels do not get used.

"Preferably one that you don't mind getting ruined?" He runs up the stairs again and returns with a stack of older towels. "Much better, thank you."

"I think your pants are ruined. Mom's gone for the night, but I could grab some of her pajamas if you would rather take a shower."

I can't help but feel a little glad, okay maybe a little more than just a little glad that our mom is gone for the night. It's not that I hate her or anything, it's just that we don't exactly see eye to eye. Some may call it the typical-mother-daughter-relationship, but what we have is far from typical. Tom and our older brother, Devin are always pushing Mom and I closer but what they don't realize is, we are both too stubborn. Dad says that may change as we get older, but I guess time will be the judge of that.

"Oh yeah? Ruined? What makes you think that?" I can tell he's trying hard not to smile at my sarcastic remark and that's why I said it. Tom is never a serious guy and when he is, it worries me. That's when I know something serious is wrong. After the crap I've been through lately, I need Jokester Tom, not Serious Tom.

"Well, I mean, there's a huge rip in them." Jokester Tom states the obvious and I laugh with him.

The peroxide rinses off most of my leg. The gash doesn't look as bad now. The antibacterial spray stings so bad that I clench my teeth and pinch my eyes shut.

"I think you need stitches!" Serious Tom points out.

"No, it's fine. Everything's fine." At this point, I'm not sure if I'm reassuring him or myself. The gash is starting to bleed again but at least it's clean. Gently, I cover it with the biggest band aid the first aid kit has to offer. This will do, for now anyways. After my body stops shuddering, I'll take a shower.

"So, what were you running from?" Tom asks while handing me a can of diet soda. This is the one thing Mom and I have in common. We both love the same soda.

"I don't want to talk about it." My favorite thing about Tom is that he never pushes for more information. He's completely content not knowing.

A few hours later, after a shower and some of Tom's famous mac and cheese I feel much better. My brain is still jumbled though. Tom went to bed almost two hours ago, but he left his laptop in the living room for me to use. I log into Myspace and since this is the only place aside from the library that I can check it, there are several new messages and a couple friend requests.

I open the messages first. Most are from obviously fake profiles, so I just delete those. One is from Tom. I still don't know why he sends me messages through Myspace when he knows I'm like never on here. I click on it anyways and it's just some glittery picture that says I should forward to ten people, otherwise, I will have ten years of bad luck. "Bring it on." I whisper to myself as I add that one to the little trash can with the others.

The last one was sent from Asher an hour ago. I hover over the bold words that read, "Please read this" but I can't bring myself to click on it. The disappointment and heartbreaking look on his face is still fresh in my mind. I decide to go back to the home page for now.

In the bulletin board, he has also posted a few surveys tonight. Normally I would read them before filling it out myself. Not tonight. Instead, I close the laptop and set it on the coffee table.

It's not long before curiosity and guilt gets the best of me, and I pick up the laptop again. I go back to the message page and before I can change my mind, I click on the bold message from Asher. Seconds into it, I'm balling.

I hope you're able to read this tonight. I hate that you left so upset. I drove around looking for you. I even stopped at your house, but your dad said he hasn't seen you. I also know that you don't have your phone since it's been ringing like crazy in your bag that was still in my car. I dropped it off with your dad by the way. I'm still not sure what happened tonight to make you react like that. I want to be able to comfort you and I'm here for you. You know that, right? Please tell me what I can do. I know you said you need some space and I just hope that didn't mean from me. But if that's what you need, I'll try to give you space, but I can't promise to wait forever.

"What am I supposed to do?" I sigh and close my eyes.

Why does my life have to be such a mess? *Mess* isn't chaotic enough to even begin describing my life. I know I should let him go. I have to, even if I don't want to. We can't keep going back and forth and I could never ask or expect him to wait, who knows how long it could take, or if it will ever get better. He needs a chance to find happiness and I need to sort things out.

Even though I've made my decision, it doesn't make it any easier. I attempt to message Asher back, but more tears begin to stream down my face. After wiping my face for what feels like the hundredth time, I start typing.

I'm sorry, Asher. I've tried to juggle everything in my life but it's obvious that I can't. You deserve more than I can give you. I think that it's time that we go our separate ways. I appreciate you more than you know and that's why I need to

do this. My life is a disaster, and I can't let it affect anyone more than it already has. I'm sorry for everything. I hope you find the happiness you deserve.

After typing and deleting for the last hour, I finally hit send. I close the laptop and set it back on the coffee table. I know I made the right decision, but I still feel like an awful person.

The cable box shows that it's almost midnight. It's peaceful here. I hope I can find a peaceful place to call home someday. I close my eyes and try to picture how my life would be if we never moved to the gray house.

I'd probably still be on the Honor Roll. Maybe I would have continued cheerleading. Gram might not have gotten so sick. I don't think Aunt Karen, David or Esther would have moved in. Jake's car certainly would not be possessed. I would most definitely be sleeping right now. The last two messages between Asher and I tonight would not have been exchanged. And I wouldn't be crying over the life I wish I had right now.

I wish we never moved to the gray house.

Chapter Twenty-Seven

Even in the quiet, I still can't sleep. I think that's the problem, It's too quiet. There is somewhere around fifty apartments in this complex, but there is no noise from the traffic, or lack thereof. But since it's now almost two in the morning, everyone else is probably sleeping anyways.

At least I'm comfortable. Mom always has the coziest pjs and blankets, not to mention, the best smelling too. I've tried using the same laundry soap but it's just not the same. The gray house plagues all good things, turning them dreadful.

As I watch the minutes slowly tick by on the cable box, I try to weigh out all of my options. Obviously, trying to ignore my problems isn't going to work. So back to plan A, burning that house down seems like a great idea still.

This has gone on for way to long. I'm ready to put an end to it. And what a better day than today?

Actually, if I start walking home now, I can grab some of Gram's stuff before anyone wakes up. I can also get home without a lot of people seeing me in these pjs. They may be comfortable, but Mickey Mouse isn't exactly my style.

"Thank you, Tom." I whisper as I slip my feet into my clean flipflops. I was too concerned about the mess I was making on the floor to even think about cleaning them. After slipping out the front door and locking it behind me, my knee starts to sting. I push through the pain and after about a mile, it doesn't hurt anymore. I'm sure I'll pay for this tomorrow, along with other repercussions.

The air feels cooler than earlier but it's still muggy, especially in these pj pants. I guess I should have asked Tom if Mom had any shorts.

The horrific gray house finally comes into view. Even from this far away. I can see a black figure standing in the purple room window. If I haven't already had so many horrific experiences and seen them myself, I might think twice about whether or not what I'm seeing is actually there.

If only *they* weren't there, this house could have some great potential.

Aside from the light above the kitchen sink, the rest of the house is dark. I pause before trying the kitchen door. It's probably locked and unfortunately Grandpa is the only one with a key. Why is it that we only have one key when there is eight of us living here? Well, usually someone is always home so that probably has something to do with it. Just as I turn to sit on the patio chair on the front porch, the kitchen door creaks open.

"Where the hell have you been?" Grandpa's voice is raspy, and I think I woke him up, even though I didn't make any noises. Grandpa has always had this odd capability to sense things. Not spiritual or demonic things, but things like me getting home shortly before the sun rises, or the way he whistles before something bad happens. Gram always says that Grandpa has always had impeccable timing too. Each night, as soon as dinner is ready, Grandpa walks through the kitchen door. His day-to-day adventures change but whether he's working, hunting, running errands, or just hanging around the house, he is always in time for dinner.

"Morning Grandpa. I'm sorry I woke you up. I stayed at Mom's last night." I decide to leave out the fact that Mom wasn't home. I already know this could go in many different ways. Gram and Grandpa don't like me walking by myself and I know I probably should have called for a ride. No matter what time it is or where I am, Grandpa is always happy to pick me up. I also should have called someone here to let them know where I was, but I didn't. Would they have even listened to me?

"You're lucky that I had to use the bathroom, otherwise you would have been sitting out here for another hour or so." Grandpa can use that as an excuse all he wants but I know he would have woken up anyways.

Once he closes the bathroom door, I head into the living room. I need to find the white box that contains Gram's little Ginny doll that she ordered from QVC forever ago. It has the cutest little dark red velvet dress and itty-bitty white ice skates. The kitchen sink light doesn't offer much light into the living room, so I pull the chain on the living room light.

"Hey man! Wanna shut that off?" Esther groans and I quickly pull the chain once more.

"Sorry." I whisper.

"Just because you can't sleep, that doesn't give you the right to wake everyone else up."

"How was I supposed to know you would be sleeping on the couch?"

"If you weren't out all night with your *boyfriend* then you would have heard the same creepy music that I heard upstairs."

"I wasn't with… Wait a minute. What did you just say?" Unsure of what I just heard Esther say, I pull the chain again. As if being able to see will make me hear better.

Esther rolls her eyes and huffs. "I said, if you weren't out all night with your…"

I shake my head. "No. You said you heard something?" She bunches her blanket up so that I can sit on the couch next to her.

"Oh. Dude, I have no idea where the music was coming from, but it sounded like one of those old wind-up music boxes. Wicked creepy! So that's why I'm sleeping down here. There's no way I could stay up there without you."

"Finally!" Finally, someone else is experiencing the unwanted too. Esther stood up for me before, but that was *before*. Now she knows firsthand that I'm not crazy.

"Well, I'm glad you think this is exciting cause I have been freaking out all night and you weren't here! Why weren't you here Emma?" Tears are now streaming down her cheeks, and I suddenly feel like a jerk.

• • •

"I'm sorry Esther! I needed some time away. I was at my mom's." Part of me, the old me who didn't mind hugs, wants to comfort her but I can't bring myself to give her one. Just sitting on this couch is suffocating enough. I try standing to see if that helps but the air just feels thick. It's this house. This house sucks the breath out of you. "And it's not that I find it exciting. I just. I mean, now you *know* that there is something going on here."

"I believed you just fine before! I don't need or want to see it!" Her fist are clenching her blanket that is now soaked from her tears.

I may not be able to comfort her physically, but maybe I can try to ease her mind. "You won't have to see it much longer." I pause from pacing, stopping directly in front of her. "I have a plan." I whisper in hopes that Grandpa doesn't hear.

"What are you talking about? What's this *plan*?"

"Nope." I say shaking my head. "That's for me to know and only me. Trust me, it's best if you don't know."

"But I could help you, Emma."

"Absolutely not." Esther is too young, and I know there's a very good possibility that I will be getting in trouble for this. I refuse to bring anyone else down with me. As long as my plan goes accordingly, everyone will be free from this place, a fresh start.

"I'm not a little kid anymore." She defends.

"I didn't say you were. This is just something that I need to take care of on my own." I begin searching for the little white box again. My eyes skim the T.V stand but it's not there. That means it's in my Grandparents' bedroom. Grandpa is outside so now's my chance.

"What are you looking for? Where are you going?" So many questions. This is why it's best if I do this on my own.

"Shh. I'll be right back." Just as I assumed though, Esther stands and follows. At least she stays quiet.

Baby is curled up under the blankets on the queen-sized bed. I wouldn't have known she was there had she not lifted her head to see who I was. Once she tucks her head back under the comforter I start glancing around and finally spot a small white box on top of the dresser. I try not to get my hopes up too much though as I pull it down. Gram is always storing stuff in random boxes, bags or anything that fits whatever she may be putting away so that she doesn't lose it. It never fails that she ends up misplacing it anyways. I lift the lid and under the tissue paper, there's Grams' Ginny doll. Just as perfect as the day she received it in the mail, thank goodness! Quickly, I replace the lid and shove it in the metal cabinet next to the kitchen door.

"What's Gram going to say when she finds out you moved her doll?"

"She's going to thank me." For not letting it burn in a fire that I planned and started. I'll keep that last part to myself though.

"Yeah, I don't think so."

Next on my list is Gram's jewelry. When I was little, I was always getting into it and Gram would get so annoyed. She was constantly hiding it in different spots so that I would leave it alone. Back then, I thought of it more like a game. Now I'm wishing that I would have just left it alone so that she wouldn't have had to hid it.

The first place I decide to check is the little cubby spot on top of their dresser. No luck. The only things in there is some random bolts. Gram probably found them laying around and put them in there so that she didn't lose them. I laugh at that thought and Esther looks at me as though I've lost my mind. Maybe I have.

Next, I wander over to the blue wooden stand with a little door covering the middle shelf. This stand has always been my favorite. When I was about seven, I convinced Gram to let me have it in my bedroom and it quickly became my favorite place to hide anything and everything. One night, we were having chop suey for dinner, and I absolutely hated that they put onions in it. So, quietly I snagged the whole bag of onions and ran upstairs to my old room and hid them in this cubby. They never did find the onions. It wasn't until they started to turn moldy and smell disgusting that I finally confessed. Ever since that day, that's the first place Gram checks when she was missing something. But of course, her jewelry isn't in there now. Nothing is.

"Why does Gram keep her old purses down there?" Esther asks while pointing to the bottom of Grandpa's wooden gun cabinet with glass doors.

"You are brilliant, Esther!" Bending down, I pull at the little brass knob and the door swings open. Grandpa never locks this, despite Gram's constant nagging. One by one I dig out Gram's old purses. She has had some interesting choices over the years. There is a small denim one, a medium sized bright red leather one, a black peeling fanny pack and a large dark blue tote bag. All are overstuffed with mail and receipts; this is Gram's version of a filing cabinet. Once a purse is filled to the point where the seams are about to burst, she gets a new one and stashes the old one down here with the rest.

"Do you think you should be snooping through those?" Esther steps back and glances at Aunt Karen and David's bedroom door.

"It's fine." I assure her but she's still looking from the door back to me. Brushing her off, I sift through the overstuffed denim purse first. After a few minutes with no luck, I set it back in the cabinet and move onto the large tote bag.

"What if Grandpa comes back inside?" I'm slightly surprised that Esther is still in here with me.

"He won't care. I'll just tell him that I'm looking for something for Gram." Technically, that's not a lie. Just as I begin to think Gram's jewelry isn't in this purse either, my fingertips brush against a zipper surrounded by denim. "Jackpot!" Without opening it, I already know that it contains exactly what I was looking for. This little bag is where Gram has stored her jewelry for at least ten years now. Once all of her bags are back where they belong, I close the little wooden framed glass door.

"What's in the bag, Emma?"

"It's best if I don't tell you." She rolls her eyes but continues following me to the kitchen. I peek out the kitchen window and Grandpa is outside but has a cup of coffee now. He must have gone up to the gas station already. I set the little bag of jewelry in the Ginny Doll box and latch the door on the metal cabinet closed.

The only two things left are Gram's massive family album and her old red bible.

Chapter Twenty-Eight

The sun is starting to rise but thanks to this immense barn attached to this side of the house, it doesn't allow much light inside. The brightness from the sunrise is nearly blinding as we step outside.

Inside the barn doesn't see much sunlight either, since the outside of the windows are covered with plywood. I find it odd that I don't sense or see anything in the barn, at least on the main floor. Maybe I should have spent more time out here instead of inside the house.

The old beams are starting to dry rot and warp. It's only a matter of time before it starts caving in. And of course, where am I? Standing right in the middle of it.

The further I go towards the back of this run-down barn, the more cautious my footing is. The wooden planks under my feet don't creek or sink but there are holes in them. Some are as small as a quarter and the biggest one so far, I could have jumped through. In the back section, the roof has started leaking so everything that Aunt Karen and David have stored out here is draped in tarps. If I was not looking for Aunt Karen's hutch, which should be the biggest item out here, then this would take forever. Who knew someone could have this much stuff? I'm no longer surprised that David had some random dog crate to give Jake.

Jake is constantly playing with the flashlights, so if we are lucky enough to find one, the batteries are usually drained or missing. Fortunately, I found this small pink one in Aunt Karen's car. It's probably David's. I don't care though, at least it works.

Standing in the middle of the dark room I try shinning the flashlight over the tarps, but the small flashlight doesn't illuminate much. Stepping over a hole big enough to swallow my foot, I notice a large rectangular shaped object under one of the tarps. This must be it. A few mice scurry out from underneath when I pull the corner of the tarp. The unforgettable dark oak wood of Karen's hutch peeks through, and I let out a breath that I had no idea I was holding. One by one I pull open the drawers and doors but all I see is random junk. Aunt Karen definitely gets that from Gram.

"Wait a second!" Tucked under some old junk mail, I can see the corner of Gram's family photo album. As I pull it out of the drawer, the junk mail falls around my feet, some of it may have slipped through the cracks in the floor. Oh well, this mess won't matter soon.

Sooner than I can close the drawer, one of the tarps across the dark room crinkles. "It's just mice." I whisper to myself even though deep down I know that sounded much bigger than a few mice. Bravely, I shine the flashlight in that direction and instantly regret it.

Standing just a few feet away, climbing through a small opening in the clutter, is a middle-aged man with tanned skin. My breath catches and my feet scramble to move but one of my flipflops get caught in a crack in the floorboards and I trip. Gram's photo album opens as it hits the floor and slides across. Pictures and little pieces of paper leave a trail to where it stops. I grip the flashlight with all I've got so that I don't drop it.

"I'm not here to hurt you." The man says with a hint of a Spanish accent. "I'm here to help you." He remains just in front of the mound of clutter, and I slowly get up on my feet. One thing that I have learned living here, is not to trust or believe anyone or anything. I need to be ready to run out of here when the timing is right. "I need your help. My family lived here fifty years ago. *He* ruined my family. I did what I could to stop *him* from hurting anyone else, but I'm guessing someone broke the seal."

"Seal? Fifty years ago? So that makes you..." Surely, he wasn't the one that put the pepper packets on the top shelf of the dumbwaiter. I have no clue as to when they were invented but something tells me that it was less than fifty years ago.

"Espiritu." Rolls off his tongue. "This house took all I had. My brother, my wife and our unborn child all suffered here. I tried to put an end to it, but nothing worked. This place is indestructible." I find that hard to believe as I stand here, on a floor that has more holes than swiss cheese.

I know part of me has been curious about the history of this place, but I'm not so sure I want to know anymore. "Why are you telling me this?"

"To stop you from making the same mistakes that I made."

"What makes you think I'm planning on doing anything?"

"You can see me, which means you can see the *others*. And I know firsthand just how cruel *they* are. Do you know how long it's been since someone was able to see me?"

I expect him to start walking towards me, but he stays in the same spot. The longer I look at him, the more he looks familiar. I feel like I've seen those eyes before. The recollection of the glowing eyes flickers but something is different. They're not filled with anger and destruction like before. There's no glow to these sad and tragic eyes. "Your eyes... I've seen you before." He shakes his head and when I see my little cousins toybox through this apparition, I'm reminded just how crazy I would look if someone walked in here right now, or if I ever told anyone about this. I should get out of here. I need to get out of here. I have things to do and right now I'm just wasting time.

"That wasn't me. I have not been in there since the day I saw mi hermano asesinato mi esposa y nuestro bebé. I knew this place was evil a few days after we arrived. My esposa loved this casa though. She had sueños of having a gran familia, which made this casa grande perfecta."

The sadness in his eyes deepen as he talks about his family, and I so badly wish that I knew more than how to count to ten in spanish. "I'm sorry but I'm not familiar with spanish."

"My apologies. One day, a month or so after my brother, my wife and I moved in, I came home from working at the Woolen Mill to the amazing news that I was going to be a father. Aina, my wife, was extático! Immediately we began working on the baby's room."

"Which room was that?" I ask hesitantly.

"*His* room, the core of this house. Hell, if you will. I didn't like the uneasy feeling that washed over me whenever I got near that room, but Aina was persistent and insisted that it would be the perfect nursery, being separated away from the rest of the house and all." He stares at the floor, deep in thought, almost as though he is reliving the recollections.

I too sit quietly and just listen. Finally, I'm getting some history on this house. And I certainly don't want to die here and end up stuck like the others. Maybe listening to his advice wouldn't be a bad idea.

"That's when we decided to move into the big room that has the door leading into the same hallway, so that we were closer to our baby's room. Something seemed off, more and more, each afternoon when I got home from work. I tried getting Aina to tell me what was going on, but she refused. When I asked Omero, my brother, if he knew what was going on..." His voice trails off and I lean forward, out of anticipation, to hear what's about to come.

"Fifty years later and I still remember it so clearly. Omero was always a gentle, caring, hardworking man. That was until we got settled in. That day something changed inside of him. Something took over him. *He* took over. Omero's eyes were like nothing I had ever seen before. They were..."

"Black." He looks up at me, full of sympathy and nods.

"And his whole demeanor was different. I suspected that he had started drinking after he quit his job the day before. I'm ashamed to say that we fought the rest of that day until he finally passed out, in the baby's room. Aina and I left and went for a walk to clear our heads. That's when she told me that we needed to move. Apparently, she had been seeing things, just as I know you have, and Omero was getting violent when I wasn't around. Even though I had never seen that side of my brother before, I knew she wouldn't lie to me. So, I promised her that we would begin packing when we got home and leave. I didn't want or need to stay any longer, Aina wanting to move out of a house that she once loved was enough for me to get us out of there that night. Even with nowhere else to go. I would figure it out. I would do anything for Aina. She was the love of my life."

"But you didn't leave, did you?"

"We did." He nods. "We packed what we could and left that night. We stayed with a guy and his family that I worked with at the Woolen Mill for a week. Aina found a house that was a little above what we could afford but we could make it work. We had to."

"So, what went wrong? Did your brother leave with you guys?"

"No, he stayed here. I tried to get him to come but he refused. We needed the money so I couldn't afford to miss anytime from work. The plan was that after I got out, my friend and I would come here and gather the rest of our stuff to bring to the new house. Omero knew where we were staying and went to see Aina. He told her that he was ready to move out as well and that he just needed her help with something at the house. My friend's wife said that she turned him down a few times before finally leaving with him. When I found out, I rushed here as fast as I could, but I was too late. Omero was holding Aina against the wall in the nursery by her throat. Her little black shoes on her feet were a good foot off the floor. I got there just in time to see her stop fighting. Her whole body went limp. When Omero turned to face me, not only were his eyes black, but it wasn't his face at all. I was beyond angry and devastated. I ran as fast as I could to save Aina. I did everything I could, but her body was lifeless. When the doctors leaned in to hear the baby's heartbeat, I knew. Part of me died that day along with the rest of my family and life."

"I am so sorry." I say between sobs and wiping the tears from my face. That is without a doubt the most heartbreaking story I have ever heard. Knowing all that happened in this house fuels my desire to burn it even more. No one else will suffer here.

"There isn't enough revenge in the world to make things even with Omero or *Him.* I remembered an old myth that my grandmother once said when I was little. You can create a seal to protect you from evil spirits by using black pepper."

"Pepper? But there's no way you were the one to scatter the pepper packets in the dumbwaiter. Or were you?"

"No, that would have been the last person who I was able to get through too. All I had were black pepper seeds, but it seemed to work well enough. Every so often it needs to be replaced though."

"Who was the last person that saw you?" With how active this place is, I can only imagine how many different families have lived here in the last fifty years.

"Your abuela." Abuela? That's Spanish for...

"Gram." But why didn't she tell me? This must be why she was so adamant about me leaving the pepper packets alone. This is why she was so against opening the upstairs. This is why she didn't seem surprised at Abigail's appearance.

"There's something that I need to tell you and I need you to listen."

If she already knew all of this before we moved here, then how the hell could she have thought this would have been a good idea? I know Gram is great at budgeting money. I find it hard to believe that she would chance going through the horrors of this house just to have cheap rent.

"Emma, I need you to listen to me. Clearly your abuela didn't, and that's why I need your full attention."

Chapter Twenty-Nine

Gram moved back here *knowing* about *him*. I thought Gram and I had an unbreakable bond. She has always been here for me. Well, maybe not right now, physically, but she is still just a phone call away or a short drive.

"If what you're saying is true, why would she move back here? Why didn't she tell me why the pepper was really there?" Gram wouldn't lie to me, would she?

I feel betrayed right now.

"This house has a way of luring people back. Maybe she had her reasons to keep this from you, but this is what you need to do."

"Hold on. If she knows how to stop him, then why didn't she do it?"

"Maybe she knows the end is near."

"The end? What the hell is that supposed to mean?" I snap and immediately feel like I have finally lost my mind. Before I know it, my feet are moving towards the entrance. There is only one person that can tell me exactly what is going on and why we moved here. Why they would move back here.

I need to talk to Gram.

"Wait!" I hear him shout as I reach the entrance.

Grandpa is picking up his box of cigars and lighter off the little white patio table on the front porch when I come out of the barn. "Emma, I was just looking for you. Your Grandmother just called, and she needs to talk to you. She didn't say…"

"That's funny because I need to talk to her as well." I brush past him and open the truck door. I'm not sure why I feel so frustrated right now, but I am. Yeah, I've been slightly annoyed with Gram from time to time but this, this feeling is new.

"David brought Jake to school, so I was heading up to see her now if you want to go."

"Emma, wait!" I hear the specter inside of the barn cry out, but I ignore him and get in Grandpa's truck. I'll find him later. He's been here for fifty years, what's another few hours?

"Grandpa, why did you guys move out of here before?" When he doesn't answer me, I glance over and he's just starting up at *that* window. My gaze follows but there is nothing there. Grandpa starts whistling and pulls out of the driveway.

"What's wrong, Grandpa?"

He nervously laughs before putting his cigar up to his lips. "Nothing."

"You're lying. You're whistling. I know somethings wrong."

"What's this? I can't whistle?" Grandpa tries to cover up his worrying but fails terribly, as I can see right through it. I have lived with my Grandparents for as long as I can remember, I know them all too well. Sometimes I think they forget that.

The walk down the overly lit wide hallway feels like it takes forever. I hate the smell of nursing homes; it reminds me too much of a hospital. Even though aside from animals, I haven't had much experience with death, that's all it makes me think of.

At last, Grandpa stops in front of Gram's room and gestures for me to go first. Instantly, I feel something is off. Gram's face doesn't light up like usual. It's almost as though she didn't see us come in.

"Hey Grammy. How are you feeling today?" Leaning over the side of her hospital bed is awkward but I give her a hug anyways. Gram doesn't even smell like herself. The familiar cucumber and melon body spray has been replaced by hand sanitizer. The smell burns my nostrils and I back away.

"Did you lock the door when you guys left the house? You checked the knobs on the stove, right? How much propane is left in the tank? We don't want to run out. Jake had a shower last night, I hope."

"Jesum crow, Rose. You are supposed to be here getting better. That's not going to happen if you keep stressing yourself out. Everything is fine at home." Grandpa assures her.

I cough and I can feel Grandpa's eyes glaring at me, warning me not to say anything. "Actually..."

"Dammit Emma. Sit down." I didn't realize I was still standing, but I don't sit, I begin pacing the small room.

"Charles, you know she has never been one to sit still. What's the matter, Emma?" Worry is smeared across Gram's face along with guilt. Something tells me that she's not worried about what's going on at home. She's worried that I now *know*. Gram has always had a way of just knowing things.

"What's the matter? Why don't you tell me, Gram?" I know this is not the time nor place for this and I feel bad for being the reason Gram is starting to get worked up again, but I'm irritated, and I need answers. "How could you move us into that house, *knowing* what was there? *Knowing* what has happened there? *Experiencing* firsthand what that house can do, what *HE CAN DO!*" My pacing quickens as I tug at my hair. I honestly can't remember that last time I felt this frustrated. "You, you put the pepper there! Why didn't you tell me, Gram? Why did you lie to me? YOU ARE SUPOSSED TO BE MY BEST FRIEND!"

Suddenly, alarms start beeping is several different sequences and tones. Before we know it, people in scrubs are filling the small room.

"Shut those alarms off and give us a few minutes!" Gram shouts over the commotion.

"Rosalie, you know we can't do that. We need to make sure you are okay." One of the ladies replies firmly. I recognize her. She was here the other times Gram had to stay in this nursing home. If I remember right, Gram likes her.

Gram scrunches her face and rolls her eyes but lets the nurse check her out anyways. This nurse gives any attitude right back to Gram. Yep, I was right. This is the one that Gram likes. By the time she gives Gram the okay, all of the others in scrubs have since cleared out.

"I was trying to protect you." Her voice is shaky, and the digital blood pressure monitor starts climbing. "I didn't tell you any of it because I was hoping you wouldn't see or experience it." My gaze shifts between Grandpa and Gram. Grandpa begins whistling and Gram wipes her eyes with a tissue. "But when you started seeing things, I knew it was too late and that we made a huge mistake."

"That's why you reacted the way you did to Simon finding the skull."

"You kids shouldn't go around touching stuff. You never know who put it there, or more importantly, why it was put there. I have always told you that I put stuff in places for a reason."

"What about Jake's little red car? You saw little Alan almost get run over because his Tonka truck told him to go play in the road. Yet, you have no problem with Jake playing with the same "imaginary friend"? Are you just waiting for the house to kill us all? Is that why you let Aunt Karen and David move in? Maybe we should invite the rest of the family to live with us. Surely the house is big enough. It could wipe us all out at once! Problem solved."

"Emma..." Grandpa cuts in.

"Or did you think that we could just pretend that we could live there as one happy family and pretend there isn't some demon trying to destroy all of us and our lives?"

"Emma, that's enough!" Grandpa commands and I finally sit because I'm exhausted and my head in spinning with too many unanswered questions. Some of which, I'm too afraid to know the answers to.

"There's no way to get rid of the spirits." Gram pauses to take a few deep breaths. I look up at the oxygen meter and they have the dial set higher than usual. "They are just stuck and until they find peace, they will remain stuck."

"Okay, but we don't have to live there and be stuck with them. You know, probably better than I do, that the spirits there will NEVER find peace. There's no way they ever could."

"This was our only option. We had to find a place to live. We will be moving once…" I cut her off before she can finish the over-used promise that no one seems capable of actually following through with.

"Would you stop saying that we are moving? I know we're not." Gram and Grandpa's mouths drop open, and I know they know that I'm right.

"We just can't find anything cheap enough." Gram and Grandpa say in unison.

"That's garbage and you both know it. That house lured you back. It's not done with us. *He's* not done with us."

Gram's face pales. "Where did you hear that?"

Grandpa abruptly stops whistling. "What were you doing in the barn this morning, Emma?"

"I was looking for something."

"I need you to promise me that you will stay out of that barn, Emma. It's not safe."

I can't stop laughing at Gram's request. "The barn isn't safe? At least I wasn't pushed down the stairs or choked with a necklace that I never put on in the barn."

Chapter Thirty

The walk back to the house is miserable but I couldn't be in that nursing home any longer. If Gram and Grandpa don't want to answer my questions, then I will have to get my answers from another source.

It must be at least a hundred degrees outside, and muggy on top of that. I've never fared well in the heat. Besides the ridiculous amounts of new freckles that appear every year, I also had heat stroke when I was younger. The fear of having that happen again scares me. Thankfully, I'm more than halfway to the gray house; now that's a thought I never expected to have.

As the house comes into view, I can't shake the mocking feeling that's creeping over me.

I hate this house more than anything in the world. Granted, I'm only almost sixteen and haven't seen much, but my hatred for this place is something I have never felt before and continues to deepen with each passing day.

The sliding barn door glides across the tracks fairly easy. The further I go, the cooler and lighter the air is. Leaning against the entryway to the back section, where I was this morning, is a collapsible camping chair. After grabbing it, I keep an eye out for the holes in the floor and cautiously set the chair up close to the same spot I was in earlier.

I'm not sure what they think is so bad about this barn. Grandpa sits just inside the entrance on hot days while he's stripping wire. I remember them telling me that Aunt Karen found Jehovah Witness books in the upstairs of the old white house in Unity that they lived in. Maybe they have this place mixed up with that place. Who knows?

"I'm going to need some answers if you don't want me going through with my initial plan of burning this horrific place to the ground." I'm not really sure how to call to a ghost besides ouija boards, and I'm still not convinced they actually work. This place is just messed up. Ouija board or not, we still would have experienced the things that plague this place.

"I know you think that's the best solution but it's not." The man's spanish accent from earlier echoes from the opposite side of the barn than where he remained. I wish I wouldn't have left the flashlight in Grandpa's truck so that I could see him better. The barn door is still open, but it doesn't offer much light all the way back here.

"Right, that's what you keep telling me. I need to know why." The only thing I can kind of see is his face. I turn my chair so that I'm facing the direction of which he is in. One of the chair legs falls into a hole as I sit down, but something stops it. Maybe the metal chair legs are too big to go through any further.

"You need to be more careful, Emma." That unforgettable deep whisper reverberates through my body, leaving chills and goosebumps behind. I hold my breath and wait. I so desperately want to run out of here, but I know I won't make it far. *He's* too close. How is *he* out here? I thought *he* was stuck inside the house.

"Emma, look at me. I need you to focus, ignore this *monstruo*. He's just trying to get to you. This place, this place is indestructible. The night my wife was killed, I tried to set fire to this house, but the flames just died."

"Just like everyone that lives here and crosses my path." *His* voice grows louder.

"There is some sort of barrier surrounding this place." He blurts and I try to listen but it's hard with a hissing sound in my ear.

"Okay, so how do we destroy that barrier?" A dark laugh sounds from behind me and my heart begins racing even faster.

"First..." He begins but, within a blink of an eye, my arms are being pulled across the dark room.

I scream as loud as I can, but my scream is muffled. My legs can't keep up and I crash into a stack of boxes. As quick as I can, I scramble to my feet.

"No te muevas." He warns and I still.

Gram knew. This is why she told me to stay out of the barn. Why couldn't she just tell me?

Slowly I brush my hands against my pants to try and brush off the dirt that I'm now covered in. A peppery fragrance fills my senses and I suddenly feel the urge to sneeze. This isn't dirt, it's pepper.

"Déjala ser. No olvidemos mi promesa a ti, una eternidad de miseria."

I have no idea what was just said but something above us slams and tumbles across the floor.

"You are safe in that spot. *He's* gone, for now." He explains weakly.

Safe? Nowhere near this property is safe.

"I thought *he* couldn't come out of the house?" My voice is a mere whisper and I begin hoping that this is just another nightmare.

"He couldn't. That was until your friends messed around with that crawl space in his room. That opened the passage."

Now that I'm further into the dark, and my eyes have had a chance to adjust, I can see this man. His light-colored shirt is stained and covered in filth. The dark colored trousers, held up by suspenders, are ripped in the knees. The simplicity and wear of his clothes take me back. I bet things were simp... "What happened to your neck?" My thoughts are cut short when my eyes catch a glimpse of the dark ring around his neck.

"I couldn't bear the thought of my esposa being stuck here with my brother and *him* for forever with no one to protect her. So, after I took care of my brother, I went upstairs..." He briefly pauses to look up at the ceiling in the barn. "And hung myself from one of the rafters."

What. The. Fuck.

"That day, I promised him an eternity of misery. I am a man of my word, Emma. I intend to do everything in my power to keep my promises. I owe this to my esposa and our unborn baby. They didn't deserve to die." The anger and frustration is clear in his voice.

Oh shit. A lump forms in my throat and I swallow hard, but it doesn't go away.

"Now that you know where I stand, I hope you understand when I say that I can't let you burn this house down. Together, we can put him back where he belongs and that is where he shall stay. But if you try to destroy this place, *he* will be the least of your worries."

Chapter Thirty-One

This is the third store that I have bought out of pepper today. As I continue placing the metal tins of black pepper on the belt, I can feel all eyes on me in this crowded store. The guy behind me in line mumbles something under his breath and I roll my eyes, almost everyone has had the same response. I don't understand why it matters to anyone else what I buy. Either way, I still have less items than everyone behind me. Letting out a deep breath, I toss the last three cans up with the others because I need all I can get, and I don't care what anyone thinks.

"Wow, this is a lot of black pepper. What are you doing with all of this?" The cashier asks with wide eyes.

"Pest control." I give her a small smile and watch her scan the rest one-by-one.

She raises one of her eyebrows. "Does it really work?"

"We're going to find out." I laugh lightly and swipe Tom's Master Card. I'm still not sure how I will repay him, but I'll figure that out another time.

As I walk into the driveway and past the barn door, I can already sense how terrible this is going to be. Before opening the door, that's directly at the bottom of the stairs, I kneel on the grass and begin tearing off the tabs that seal the pepper containers. I want to be as prepared as I can be. I still have no idea just how many I bought but I hope five bags full is suffice.

"Seventy-two." I count. Seventy-two cans is exactly how many I have. This should be enough, right? I guess I will see.

My emotions stir when I push the door open, and Abigail is standing at the top of the stairs. I so desperately want to know this poor little girl's story. Why is she stuck here? What happened to her hand? How did she die and how long ago? Judging by the style of her dress, I'm assuming it was probably back in the 1800's. That's a long time to be trapped here, in *this* house.

With each step I take closer to her, her face saddens more and more. I take a deep breath as I reach the nineth step and she still hasn't moved. The pepper container in my hand is already open. Should I start sprinkling it now? Will that get her to move?

Keeping my eyes on her, I start shaking the pepper on the next step, and the next, and the next.

"No!" She shrieks so loud that I cover my ears, dropping the pepper. "STOP!"

After the ear-piercing shriek ends, I quickly snatch up the small tin off the step ahead of me. Holding off sprinkling any more, I decide this may be my chance to find out more about her.

"What happened to you?" When she doesn't answer, I shake the can a little. Pepper coats the next step and I take another step closer.

"When did your family live here?" She shakes her head and I coat the next stair.

I'm almost at the top of the stairs and she still hasn't moved. A door thumps and ricochets off a wall, making me jump. I don't have to look to know it's the creepy room door. Grasping the small tin in my hand harder, I reach for a second can. I wish I would have dumped them all in a bucket.

"What happened to the rest of your family? Are they still trapped here too?"

"This is my family's house. They built it." She mumbles.

All I can hear is the blood pulsing in my ears, making it difficult to hear what she's saying. Did she say her family built this house?

"That's a long time to be trapped here. Why haven't you been able to move on?" She shakes her head again and I empty the remainder of the can on the last step. I'm now face to face with her, just inches between us.

"Ma and Pa called me a disappointment!" She cries. "They even built my room so no one would see me, but you see me!" Her head tilts to one side and footsteps resonate beside me from the long narrow hallway. "How?"

"I... I don't know." I wish I knew.

"Help me!" She pleads.

"I want to, I do, but you have to tell me how."

"No one can help her!" A deep growl overtakes the pulsing in my ears.

Towering behind Abby is a dark mass. My chest tightens as his black eyes meet mine.

"Don't listen to him." A raspy but feminine voice interrupts. I turn towards it, and it's the older lady in the wheelchair. "*We* may not have a chance to escape his grasp and find peace but *you, you* still have a chance. The rest of us are the victims. *His* victims. Abigail and I can't let you become one of us."

"Quiet, Velma!" *He* hisses.

As much as I want to scream and run far away from this place, I can't let them win. I can't let *him* win. I turn back to face Abigail, and she takes a step back, finally. I straighten my shoulders and pour more pepper at my feet.

Laughter echoes around me. I panic and throw the rest of the can in my hand at Abigail. Effectively, she moves back but the laughter continues to grow louder.

"Can't you see, little girl? This house is just a trap. Its grand appearance lures you in, it lured all of us in. Not all of us get to leave though." Velma glares at the dark mass and chills consume me. "You," Her gaze is back to me. "Up until now, *you could have still left.*"

Could have still left? "What the hell is that supposed to mean?"

"Darling, you're about to be stuck here with the rest of us." Velma's sweet tone is condescending.

Heavy footsteps echo off the walls and within seconds I'm surrounded and blocked. My chest feels heavy as fear starts taking over. What was I thinking? I can't do this by myself. I need help. I'm not ready for this. My eyes shift to the door at the bottom of the stairs. If this pepper actually works, then I should be able to run down the stairs.

"Don't even think about it." A livid voice sounds in my ear. "I have a lot of mistakes to make up for, Emma. Luckily, for all of us, I have an eternity to right my wrongs." Omero warns.

"I... I'm not sure how... killing me would help you make up for anything." In attempt to swallow my fear, I straighten, and pop open the next can. I'm not dying today.

"Abigail enjoys your company." *He* confesses. "She's never had friends and that's my own fault. I was too ashamed and embarrassed of her appearance to let anyone too close. That's why my wife and I built this estate here. We hoped Abigail would be satisfied with just seeing the city, but she needed more. More than I was prepared to give her. I failed her back then and I will not fail her now." *He* says out of desperation.

"My father is correct." Abigail gleams at *him*.

"Father?" My heart pounds. There's no way this sweet girl is *his* daughter.

Omero takes another step closer. "Emma, there is something about you. You're different. You belong here. Rose was right to bring you here."

Suddenly, the hallway is spinning. How is Abigail his daughter? "No. No. NO!" I refuse to die in in this hell hole. Frantically, I shake the tins of pepper. The guy with the ball and chain attached to his ankle is the first to disappear from his usual spot just inside the doorway of the pink room. Something burns my thigh through my jeans. Reaching into my pocket, my fingers touch hot metal. I forgot I had Jake's little red car. Quickly, I toss it down the narrow hallway. It lands a foot or so away from the creepy room door.

"You can't do this, Emma! I thought you were different! I thought you cared about me!" Abigail shouts, making my heart break for her. I know she doesn't deserve this, but I need to protect my family, even if they could care less.

Tossing the empty tins as I go, I continue pouring the pepper onto the floor. At last, I have them cornered in the red room and the entrance to the creepy room. Glowing eyes peer around the corner in the hallway. *Omero*. I hope Aina was able to move on from this place. I haven't seen her yet and that gives me hope.

"Please don't do this!" Abigail cries out and I try to ignore her. "Father, make this stop!"

His eyes are locked on mine as he starts towards me. I don't have to look down to know that I'm safe, well as safe as I could be. There is a good three feet of pepper surrounding me.

"You don't know what you're doing! This won't end us."

"I know that, but until I can figure out how to end all of this, this will at least keep my family safe for now." Panic starts to creep inside me when I only feel a few more tins in the bag. I still have to coat half of the red room. How did I already use almost seventy cans? I'm so close though. "Abigail, I'm sorry. I know you don't deserve this, but I have to keep my family safe."

"You may think you know everything, but you're wrong." Dark eyes glare at me as I shake the tin a little more. "I don't just possess that room. I possess anything and anyone. You can trap us in this room but someday, you will be back. They always come back." Standing in the center of the creepy room, Abigail's eyes darken as I pour out the last tin of pepper in the threshold of her room and shut the door.

Leaning against the wall of the narrow hallway, I let out a deep breath of relief. Screams come from the other side of the door, but I barely hear them through the ringing in my ears. Once again, the hall starts spinning. My knees weaken and everything goes black.

Chapter Thirty-Two

It's been a week since I woke up on the floor, just outside of Abigail's room, covered in black pepper. It's like that whole day has been set on repeat in my mind. I thought I was at my breaking point before, but now? Now I'm at a loss. I feel numb. I don't have it in me to feel anything else. I never should have stepped foot into the barn. I should have just burned this place.

This has been the quietest six days of my entire life. I'm just standing here, at the end of the long narrow hallway. The red crap oozing down the wall has stopped and is slowing turning brown as it finally dries. Seventy-two. Seventy-two empty black pepper containers remain scattered across the floor from seven days ago. Maybe someday I will have the energy to pick them up. Today is not that day. Tomorrow probably won't be either.

The creepy room door has stayed closed for exactly six days.

I haven't seen Abigail in six days, not even in the window.

There has been no stomping or slamming doors for six days.

Apparently six days has also been enough time for my bruises to finally go away. Well, aside from the handprints on my forearms from when I was pulled across the room in the barn. Those are yellow now and almost gone.

I'm just waiting for the next blow. Dowsing the house in pepper couldn't have been all it took to put *them* away.

"Emmy! Grammy is home! Come on!" Jake shouts from the bottom of the stairs, breaking my trance.

I'm glad that Gram coming home has him this excited. He's been lost without his little red car. I may or may not have kicked that inside the creepy room before I sealed it off. I know he has a beguiling bond with it, but this is for his own good. I feel slightly guilty when I hear him wake up crying in the middle of the night because he still can't find it. Sometimes I pretend to help him look for it, but that just brings on more disappointment when we don't find it. Eventually he will move on. Hopefully, someday we all will. I'm not holding my breath since I know it will be a long time from now.

Is all of this something we will ever be able to move on from?

"Emma, your grandmother needs your help getting situated!" Dad yells up the stairwell on his way from his bedroom to the living room.

"I'll be down in a minute." I'm not sure if I was even loud enough for him to hear me but I know that I have a few minutes until he yells for me again.

I just need a few more minutes.

At least that's what I've been telling myself for the last six days. The absolute quiet is deafening and for some reason, I can't stop staring down this hallway at the white door. Even though I haven't seen so much as a shadow or any movement through the gap under the door for six days, this door is still creepy. It always will be.

"Dude, you should be happy instead of standing here, staring at that damn door." Esther grips my shoulders and turns me around so that we are both facing the stairs. She has done this several times over the last seven days. By day four I finally stopped freaking out at her. I still cringe when her hands touch my shoulders but it's no longer such a constricting feeling. "Are you hoping that things start happening again?"

"Of course not!"

"Alright then, let's go see Gram." Esther's right, the longer I stand here and stare at this damn door, the more likely something is to manifest. Or I'll lose what little sanity I have left.

One step at a time, we make our way down the stairs. Even the stairs don't creak like they did a week ago.

"There you are! Your grandfather just went to pick up my new prescriptions but when he gets back, I need you to sort them for me. You know, in the case for the week?" Gram says more irritated than usual.

"I can do that. How are you feeling?" Gram looks so much better than she did when I last saw her, a week ago. *That* probably has something to do with her irritation. I just couldn't bring myself to go back. I already stressed her out that last time I visited. Secretly, I'm hoping that she has had plenty of time to forget about that day.

"Well enough for them to finally let me leave. Come here and let me kiss your head since I didn't get to before you stormed out of my room." I should have known she wouldn't have forgotten. Gram never forgets. She still brings up some floral embroidered towels that apparently my mom has that are hers, from almost sixteen years ago. I highly doubt Mom still has them, that was a long time ago.

Cautiously, I take a deep breath and lean forward. After she kisses the top of my head, I'm quick to stand back up. I miss the days when I just wanted to cuddle with Gram all day. Unfortunately, I doubt that will be able to happen again anytime soon.

"Can you start some coffee?"

"Are you supposed to have coffee, Gram?" If I remember correctly, coffee is at the top of the last avoid list that she was sent home with. Each time a new list is sent with her, so maybe she can have it now?

"A little bit won't hurt me, Emma. I'm sixty-five, if I want a cup of coffee, I will have a cup of coffee. That's the same thing I told them in the nursing home."

"If you say so. How many scoops for half a pot?"

"Two but don't forget, your grandfather and Baby will have some too. You better make a full pot to be safe." If Gram doesn't give her little white and black yippy dog some coffee too, Baby will climb up and drink Gram's right out of her cup. Just like

Arliss and his dog Old Yeller. It's kind of funny that this happens to be one of Gram's favorite movies. It doesn't make it any less repulsive though.

"Four scoops it is."

"Grammy! You see my car?" Jake whines and climbs into Gram's lap. I know he's getting too heavy to be climbing on her, I go to grab him, but Gram shakes her head at me and wraps her slim arms around him even tighter.

Gram glares over the top of her glasses at me. "You still haven't found it?"

"I've been trying to help him find it." I shrug my shoulders and get back to starting the coffee. I can't see how people can actually drink this stuff. It smells awful and tastes even worse. Gram and Grandpa say that I'll like it when I get older. However, Dad says it's okay that I don't like it now because it could stunt my growth. I'm just barely five-foot-three now, so I guess I shouldn't chance it.

"Have you checked on the back porch? How about in your father's truck? Jake, did you bring it to school?" Somehow Gram always knows where things are without actually looking for them. Except for the things that she puts in special places. Those things are forever lost.

"It's nowhere, Grammy!" Tears start welling up in his little eyes and guilt sneaks over me, once again.

"We've looked everywhere. It's nowhere to be found." That's not exactly a lie. It's just in a place that no one will find it.

* * *

"Jake, why don't you hook Baby outside and go see what your father is doing?"

"Okay! Let's go Baby!" Of course, Baby is all excited. Her little curly tail shakes back and forth while she jumps around on her back legs. Jake's laughing now and a small smile forms across Gram's face.

No sooner does Jake close the door, Gram's smile fades as she asks the question that I thought I already dodged.

"Where is Jake's car?"

"Jake is better off without it." I defend.

"Emma, I won't ask you again, where is Jake's car? I think we have already irritated the spirits in this house enough. What did you do?"

"Don't worry, I put it away somewhere safe. Why didn't you tell me about the guy in the barn?" Two can play this game.

"I tried to tell you."

"No. You told me to stay out of the barn. You didn't tell me why or that *you* also talked to the same guy back when you guys lived here before? Why didn't you tell me? I thought we told each other everything?"

Gram shakes her head. "Gustavo isn't who you think he is. He's no better than the other ones." She pauses and points at the kitchen ceiling, where the creepy room is. "He killed his own brother. You have no idea what he is capable of."

"His brother killed his wife and unborn child! Of course, he's going to be mad! He has every right to be. Woah. Wait… He…

he what?" Why didn't he tell me that part? Surely, he had plenty of chances. Something switches inside my head. The feeling to defend this strange ghost from the barn vanishes.

"I'm telling you, he's not just mad. He's looking for revenge. An eternity of revenge. Did he tell you how many innocent people have died in this house because he coaxed them into the trap?"

"Innocent people? What trap?" He told me that the last person he spoke to was Gram. That would have been about twenty years ago and if he's only been here for the last fifty...

"Your Uncle Alan's old train room. Something demonic possesses that room and always will. Gustavo doesn't care about anything or anyone. As long as this house stands, he will continue using innocent people to close off that room. That's when people usually get sucked into the trap and they never leave. I was almost one of those people, you know."

With this house being built in 1820, that's almost one hundred and eighty-five years. I can feel the color draining from my face before I can even ask my next question. "How many people have died here?" Gram's eyes dart to the floor and I immediately regret asking.

"Oh, I don't know exactly." She begins picking at her already chipped nail polish and I know this is her way of avoiding the real answer.

"Gram." I try to recollect how many I have seen since we opened the upstairs. "There's *him* and Abigail in the creepy room. Whatever possesses Jake's little red car is probably the same thing that possessed little Alan's Tonka truck. Gustavo is in the barn. Omero and his glowing eyes are upstairs in the hallway. There's some guy with a ball and chain attached to his ankle in the little pink room. And the only other one I have seen is an elderly lady in a wheelchair, usually in Uncle Alan's old bedroom."

Gram's hand begins trembling and her coffee splashes out of her cup, onto her white t-shirt. "That's not even a quarter of them. Sealing off that room is just a band aid. Sooner or later, it's going to get ripped off like one as well."

A quarter of them? If that's the case, I'm even more confused as to why Gram would ever think about stepping foot into this house again, never mind living here again. "Why did you come back here? Why the hell are we here!?"

"Guilty conscience, I guess. If I would have known that this house was going to be sold as soon as it was, we would not have moved here. The new owners are planning to tear this whole place down as soon as we move out. They want to build a restaurant in what is now the backyard. I doubt they will be able to because of it being considered a flood zone but as long as they tear it down, I could care less what they do with the property. I just hope I'm still around to see it destroyed."

More so than before I'm realizing the enormity of not just this house but also its occupants and their history. Brief thoughts of burning this place to the ground come back. That seems like a more permanent solution. If the landlord is going to tear it down anyways, maybe he will thank me instead of pressing charges.

Right now, a windy day with all of the windows open up stairs would easily destroy this pepper remedy. I need to find something better and soon.

Chapter Thirty-Three

The last few weeks have been a blessing. The house is still peaceful. Esther has moved into her own room, but still spends most of her time in mine. I don't mind though; she's become the sister I never knew I wanted. Jake has a new obsession with Pokémon cards, so he no longer cares about his little red car. Aunt Karen and David have started looking for another place to live. Gram has been doing okay, less stress helps. Her health problems won't get any better but at least she is still here with us. We have fallen into a nice routine and thanks to my dad agreeing to let me homeschool, I no longer have to worry about actually going to school. Not that I would have the time to go anyways, now that I'm working fulltime to help save some money, so that we can get out of this dreadful house.

When I walk into the kitchen, Gram's sitting at the kitchen table, wiping it off with a towel. I offered to clean it for her, but she stuck her tongue out at me and shook her head. I can't imagine how hard it has been for her since she got really ill. She's always done all of the cooking and cleaning, but now she has to sit back and instruct others. Sometimes this can be quite interesting to watch.

• • •

"Alright Gram, your medicine is all set, and the visiting nurse should be here soon. Is there anything else you need before I head to work?"

"What time is the visiting nurse coming?" Gram may sound irritated about the nurse coming but it's only because she gets anxious when she knows people are coming over, it doesn't matter who it is. I know it's comforting for her at the same time though. It's certainly comforting to me; knowing that someone will be here with her while I'm at work.

I peek at the clock again. "Seven. So, in about fifteen minutes."

"Are you sure you don't want to do anything for your birthday?"

"Yes Gram, I'm sure. We have more than enough going on. It's just another day. Besides, I'm sure I'll have to work." I'm just not in the mood for it this year. I know this is hard for Gram. She has always made sure that us grandkids have had a birthday party. Our first year in this house, she sent Marie and I to the store to get an ice cream cake and food to cook on the grill. When we got back, the back porch was decorated for Marie's birthday. We both thought that's what Gram was up to, but we didn't want to ruin the excitement for her.

"If you say so. Where have your friends with the cars been?" Is this some sort of trick question? She always used to get so nervous about me riding with teen drivers. Well, besides Asher.

* * *

"I have no idea; I think you really scared Collin and Preston the one and only time they came over. And I just haven't wanted to hang out with anyone."

"What about Asher?" Have I not told her?

"Oh. We broke up. I don't have time to talk about it now." I also don't *want* to talk about it. There's not much to discuss anyways. From what I've heard, he has a new girlfriend and honestly, I'm happy for him. She's beautiful, sweet and I bet she has a lot less responsibilities. I may be slightly envious, but I wish them the best.

"Fine but promise me that you will call your friends, you know, the ones with the cars? Not that other one that went into that room. You have been through more than any teenager should ever have to and you deserve to have some fun."

"Is this reverse psychology or something?"

"No Emma. This is not some evil plot against you, I just want to see you smile again."

I plaster the biggest and least convincible smile across my face. She shakes head and rolls her eyes but starts laughing, and so do I. "I love you Grammy. Good luck with the nurse and be nice to whoever it may be."

"Of course, I will be. What kind of person do you think I am?" Oh, I know exactly what kind of sassy, loving, angry, caring, smartass, nurturing, frustrating and amazing woman she is. "As long as it's not *that* one. You know which one I'm talking about. She couldn't even get the blood pressure cuff on!"

"Gram! That's probably because you made her so anxious! Give these women a break. You were an LNA for many years. So, you should know how much crap, literally, that they deal with."

"Maybe you should stay home with me today."

Here we go. This is the same thing she would do nearly every morning before school. Most days, I'd cave and spend the day with her. I wish she would have mentioned this earlier instead of twenty minutes before I have to punch in.

"It's too late for me to call out, I have to go. Everything will be fine, just be nice. I'll call you when I go on break." Leaning forward, I beat her to it and kiss the top of her head. She smells like Juicy Fruit and her signature cucumber and melon body spray. Besides some overly priced Avon perfume that she used to use when I was little, this is how Gram always smells and for a brief second, I feel at peace.

During my walk to work, I think about what Gram said. It has been a long time since I've actually smiled. I guess there just hasn't been any reason too. Maybe I will see what Collin and Preston are up to. Their unusual sense of humor could make anyone laugh. Reaching into my pocket, I pull out my phone and send a quick text to Collin.

What are you guys up to? Wanna hang out later?

After I hit send, I slide my phone back into my pocket, since I know he won't respond anytime soon. The rest of the walk to work only takes about ten minutes and just as I reach the time clock, my phone dings.

What are you doing now?

Working.

Quit. Come hang out with us.

Can't.

Can.

The thought seems appealing, but I can't, I need the money. With my timecard already in my hand, I sigh and silent my phone. I'm out at four today anyways. That's early enough to check in with Gram, change my clothes and make it out of the house before Esther talks me into staying.

Work dragged and I swear, the smell of dill and vinegar is forever burned into my nostrils. I still can't believe I dropped a huge jar of pickles on the floor. I'm definitely going to need a shower before I go anywhere.

"How was work? Are you hungry?" David asks as soon as I close the kitchen door. He's stirring something on the stove in a big pot. Whatever it is smells terrible but thank goodness I don't have to cook dinner tonight.

"Wonderfully." I say sarcastically and glance down at my still-wet-sneakers. They have had some time to dry but they still feel wet and uncomfortable. The bottom of my pants are almost dry, but I still smell awful. I don't think I'm getting this smell off me anytime soon. "No thank you."

"Oh my, Emma. Why do you smell like pickles?" Aunt Karen's pinching her nose and within seconds, Gram, David, Jake, and Dad are doing the same.

"I don't smell anything." Grandpa says before heading outside.

"Dad, how do you not smell that?" Aunt Karen starts gagging and goes into the living room to put some space between us.

I follow behind her, only because I need to get upstairs to get a change of clothes and a towel so that I can finally get rid of this smell. Aunt Karen turns into Gram and Grandpa's room. I can't help but laugh when I hear her take a deep breath.

"Oh, come on, Aunt Karen! It could be worse!" I shout as I run up the stairs. Actually, whatever David is cooking *does* smell worse.

Everything upstairs is just as I left it this morning. I kind of like that it's just Esther and I up here. We both like our stuff to be left alone and our space. The last month has been perfect up here. There was even one night that I slept a decent seven hours straight. I haven't dared shut the lights off, but at least I got some sleep.

"Emma? Please tell me that's you!" Esther yells from her room as I run past the *now* brown dried up crud on the wall.

"It is!" I yell back.

No sooner do I swing my bedroom door closed, it swings open and when I spin around, Esther is standing just inside the doorway, pale and out of breath.

Chapter Thirty-Four

Esther is freaking me out. She's pacing in my room and I'm just standing here, waiting for her to tell me what the hell is wrong.

This is what I get for thinking today could be as simple as working, checking on Gram, changing and leaving. No, instead work sucked. I desperately need a shower. And now, Esther is having a melt down and I have no clue why.

I should probably cancel my plans. Clearly, it's going to be awhile before I'll be able to leave.

"So, I was talking to my sister on the phone, and I started hearing music!"

"Music?" We both love music, and an extensive variety. I don't understand why she would be this flustered from hearing music.

"It was wicked creepy!"

"Okay? Was your sister listening to music? I'm not following. Where was the music coming from?"

"No Emma! It was coming from the pink room!"

"What kind of music? Maybe it's just from something Jake was watching?" I'm not trying to belittle her; I'm just holding on to the last bit of hope that I have.

"It was most definitely coming from the pink room. I swear, Emma! It sounded like an old music box. Like the ones that you have to wind-up."

I shake my head. *That's not possible.*

"Trust me, I wouldn't be telling you if I wasn't sure."

"Maybe it was coming from the creepy room." Not that that makes it any more comforting, but I wouldn't be a bit surprised if it were. The way I see it, is that they can make as much noise as they want, as long as they stay in the creepy room.

"Well, yeah I mean I guess it could have been coming from there." Color is slowly returning to her face, and she looks a little more relaxed.

"Let's go check it out. I just have to grab my clothes." Shuffling through the basket of clean clothes, that I have yet to put away, I pull out a pair of jeans, a tank top and a sweater. Since it's still really warm out, I normally wouldn't worry about a sweater, but I never know what kind of adventure Collin and Preston have in mind.

"Where are you going?"

"To the pink room?" I question while closing my sock drawer.

"Obviously. I mean after?"

• • •

"Just out for a little bit."

Esther keeps her distance as she follows me down the hallway. I take a deep breath before peeking down the narrow hallway. The white door at the end is still closed and the empty pepper containers are still where I dropped them; scattered across the floor. The only sound I hear is our footsteps and some pigeons that have started to make homes in the eves. I believe Esther but I don't hear any music. Gram always says that ghosts only make themselves known if they sense you are ready to see them. I'm not so sure I believe that anymore. I can't imagine anyone could ever be prepared or ready to see what I have in this house.

Something else that Gram said clicks.

That's not even a quarter of them. Sealing off that room is just a band aid.

Could this be something new trying to manifest? If so, I'm not sure I'm ready for this either. That eerie feeling is back. Goosebumps creep down my arms. I so badly just want to run downstairs.

"Emma?" Esther's voice is much quieter than usual.

I still don't hear anything. "Do you hear any music now?" After another deep breath, I step into the doorway of the pink room. With no windows, it's fairly dark except for the little bit of light beaming in from Esther's room across the hall. From what I can see, the small room appears empty.

"No, but can you just stay and listen for a few minutes?" I pull out my phone to check the time, I've already been out of work for an hour, and I haven't even showered yet.

Maybe I *should* have called out today, then maybe, it wouldn't have been a complete disaster. I definitely wouldn't smell like pickles right now.

"Just for a few minutes. I'm sorry, Esther. It's just that I finally made plans and I've actually been looking forward to them."

"Just another minute. I have plans too. I'm going to my sisters for the weekend. She should be here any minute to pick me up."

Silently, we wait for another minute and neither one of us hear anything. I continue waiting while Esther scrambles around her room shoving clothes into her backpack. Once she grabs her MP3 player and headphones off her dresser, I know she's all set. Still not hearing anything but the pigeons cooing, I follow her to the stairs.

"Oh hey, I would shower if I were you. You smell disgusting!" She says as we race down the stairs like we have been for the past two weeks, but tonight, the stairs sound louder. That creaking sound is back.

I hold up my towel. "I plan to. It's been a crappy day." I have a sudden urge to stay home again but I refuse to cave in. This house has taken far too much of my time. I send Collin a quick message to let him know I will be ready in about fifteen minutes.

"Well, I hope you have fun tonight, Emma. And I mean actual fun. Push everything in your mind to the side and let yourself enjoy whatever it is that you're doing tonight." For being a few years younger than me, Esther is actually really good at giving advice.

At last, I'm out of the house, and no longer smell like pickles. Or maybe I still do but I'm used to it now. Gram's only reminder was to wear my seatbelt, which is unusual, and I find it odd, but I'm not going to dwell on it. I start walking up the sidewalk to the parking lot where I'm supposed to meet Collin and Preston when I hear someone running behind me. I move towards the edge so that they can pass me but the footsteps slow, matching my pace.

"Excuse me." A deep breathless voice says next to me. "Do you have any money?"

My heart races. This is exactly what Gram has spent my whole life warning me about. I shake my head and pick up the pace.

"Are you sure?" Now that this man has had a chance to catch his breath, his voice sounds familiar, but I can't pinpoint why. I want to see who it is, but I continue looking forward, I've watched too many Lifetime movies where someone ends up dead just because they saw the murderers face. "Come on, Emma."

How the hell does this man know my name? Keeping my gaze forward, towards the parking lot isn't easy. I start walking a little faster. The footsteps next to me increase as well. *Shit*. This is as fast as I can walk before it turns into running.

"You must have an extra dollar." His hand firmly grips my shoulder and I scream as loud as I can.

"Leave me alone!"

Collin's car pulls into the parking lot, and I run, not stopping until I reach it.

"Dude, is that man following you?" Preston asks as he opens the passenger door so that I can climb into the back seat.

"I'm not sure if I would call it following but he wanted money." My hands are shaking, and my lungs feel like they are filled with needles with each breath I take. *What if they didn't show up when they did?*

"Do you know him?" Collin snuffs his cigarette out in the ashtray while keeping his eyes on the man continuing in our direction.

Leaning between the two front seats to get a better look, I can see that the straggly man must be around my dad's age, but I don't recognize him. "No, but he knew my name. Maybe he's a friend of my dad." Not that that's anymore reassuring. Since moving into the gray house, Dad has made friends with everyone he sees walk by.

Collin and Preston look at each other in silence. The sunroof begins to open while Preston digs into the middle console. He pulls his hand out and it's full of coins. After tossing a few back in, he chucks them through the sunroof. The clinging of coins hitting the pavement echoes through the empty parking lot. The straggly man glances at the coins but continues walking towards us.

"Dude, we should probably leave." Preston snickers.

Collin looks back at me and I nod. "I agree." I don't want anyone to fight, I just want to get far away from this strange guy and never see him again.

"Fine." Collin squeals out of the parking lot as I rush to buckle.

The warm night air is calming as it rushes through the windows. The needles in my lungs have dulled and with each deep breath, so has my anxiety.

"What are we doing tonight?" I ask when the song ends. I will say, Collin has the best taste for music. I never know what genre to expect and most of it, I've never heard before.

"What do *you* want to do?" A techno song starts before I can answer. I take this time to think of something for us to do. It's been a long time since I've hung out with them, so I have no idea what they do for fun anymore.

When one of them turns the music down, I know they are awaiting my answer. "What do you guys usually do?"

Preston chuckles and starts snapping his fingers. "We could go out to Unity!"

"Emma, you know anyone else that wants to hang out?"

"Preferably someone single and hot?" Preston adds.

"Word!"

"You guys are something else." I laugh. "I don't have any friends." Thanks to the gray house.

"Lies!" They shout at the same time.

"Esther is at her sister's house for the weekend. I guess I could see what Olivia is up to?"

"Yes, yes you should."

The little screen on my phone seems brighter than usual in the back of this car. Tilting it to the side kind of helps. I send Olivia a text and since she is always quick to respond, I keep my phone open in my hand.

"So, what's in Unity?" I ask. They both turn around towards me. After glancing at each other for a moment I add, "Don't judge! I've been out of the loop for a while. I have no idea what anyone does for fun anymore!"

"Not much changes around here."

"Seriously though, Unity is where it's at! Camping."

"No cops."

"The flats."

"No cops." Collin repeats.

"You said that." I point out and Collin just grins. My phone dings, it's Olivia.

What are you guys doing?

I'm not sure yet.

Let me ask my mom. Meet me at the gas station?

Okay.

"Oh! Oh!" Preston is all sorts of excited about whatever he's thinking about. "There's also some old ass house that we could go check out! I've heard it's pretty cool."

"Or we could not." Anything would be better than that.

"Hey! You live in a house that's probably just as old, if not older."

"What are you, scurd?" Clucking noises start filling the car until we're all laughing too hard.

Scared? Oh no, I'm not scared of much anymore. It's just that tonight was supposed to give me a break from creepy old houses. "Olivia said to meet her at that gas station next to her house."

Olivia hops off the picnic table when we pull into the gas station. As she approaches Preston's door, he starts to roll down his window and before he can tell her to go to the other side, I start moving over.

"It's fine, Preston. I can just move over."

"Hey guys!" Olivia climbs in next to me.

"Hey guys!" Collin and Preston mock.

"Hey Olivia." I smile. Tonight, may not be so bad after all.

Chapter Thirty-Five

Just as I expected, Gram's sitting in her usual spot at the kitchen table. "Well, did you have a good time last night?"

A *good* time? I'm not exactly sure if I would refer to it as a *good* time. As I contemplate my answer, Gram's smile fades. "It was alright." I say quickly before she can overthink letting me go out for the night.

"What happened? I mean, what did you kids do?" She corrects herself.

"We just picked up Olivia and drove around." At the mention of Olivia's name, Gram relaxes a little.

"Did you at least have some fun?"

Visions of Collin, Preston, Olivia, and I running as fast as we could down the treacherous-overgrown-driveway come back. "Yeah, I had some fun." Everything leading up to the Unity house was fun. After, is a completely different story. "Just out of curiosity, where was that house that you guys used to live in? The one in Unity."

"On the flats, across the street from the farm. Why? You kids better not be fooling around up there!"

"Was it white?"

"Emma."

"I'm just asking Gram."

"Yes, it was. Why are you asking about it?"

"Just curious."

"The spirits there are nothing like the ones here. But don't go provoking them!"

"Trust me, I don't plan to." After everything that's happened in this house, I'll be damned if I ever mess with the other side again.

Gram clasps her hands together and grins slightly. "Good. Now, do you *have* to work today?"

I already know what she's getting at. "A relaxing day of hooky is just what I need, Gram." Today is my day off anyways, but I'll let her believe what she wants. Skipping school to spend days with Gram was always worth it. "What are our plans today?"

Her face lights up as she points to the metal cabinet behind me. "I was hoping you would say that! I asked your grandfather to pick up some of those rice packets. They are in there. Along with another treat."

Opening the cabinet, tucked in the corner on the top shelf is a packet of chicken and broccoli rice and an opened container of strawberry filled pastry puffs. Grandpa loves these,

I have no doubt that he was the one who opened them. "You and I are the only ones who eat this rice, Gram. You really don't have to hide it."

"You never know in this house." She has a valid point.

"How about I cook the rice while you think about what to watch?"

"There's a Little House on the Prairie marathon playing today that we can watch."

"You really have this planned out, don't you?"

"I always do, Emmy."

Chapter Thirty-Six

"Emma! Emma! Come see this! Hurry up or else you're going to miss it!"

Grabbing the dish towel next to the kitchen sink, I run to the living room. Gram's face is practically glowing from excitement. She's pointing at something on T.V but I can't look away. I've always thought Gram was beautiful, but when I try to tell her she brushes it off. She may see white hair that needs to be dyed. Scars from when she had the measles back when she was seven. Or a weathered body that's ruined with wrinkles. But all I see is a beautiful woman. My Gram isn't just my Gram. She's also my best friend, my mentor, my therapist... my everything.

"Emma! Did you see that dress? I think it would look beautiful on you. Once I get enough money, I'm going to order it. It's in women sizing, what do you think, should I get you a small?"

"Oh, yeah Gram, you're...it's beautiful." I have no idea what the dress on QVC looks like and I know she won't take no for an answer, so agreeing is the best route to take. The dress

probably isn't my style, but seeing her smile grow makes it worth it.

"What are you looking at? All my wrinkles? Do I have something on my face? I know I need to dye my hair..."

I shake my head and smile, despite the tears streaming down my face. "I love you Grammy."

"Come over here, so I can kiss the top of your head." Her arms may be thin, but her hugs always feel like a blanket of comfort. "I love you, Emmy."

My eyes jolt open, and my heart is pounding. Slowly, I sit up, allowing my legs to hang off the edge of the bed. As my eyes start to focus, I can see that I'm in my bedroom. What time is it? Where is my phone? I grab my pillow to see if my phone is under it. My pillow is drenched. Have I been crying? As my fingers touch my cheeks, I realize that I'm still crying. *Something's wrong.*

Uneven footsteps sound in the hallway. My heart beats harder with each one. Without a knock, my door swings open. *Something's wrong.*

Grandpa's eyes are watery and red. His hands grip the door casing as he struggles to hold himself up and take a breath. "I... I need you to... to come wake your grandmother up. I... I tried but..." Tears flood his eyes. "But she won't wake up!"

No. No. No. This can't be happening. Flashbacks of my dream come to me as I run down the stairs like never before. In the living room, Dad and Jake are standing next to Gram's hospital bed. Unintentionally, I push them out of the way so that I can reach her.

"Gram?" I touch her shoulder and wait for her eyes to open, but they don't. "Grammy, please wake up!" With all I've got, I shake her frantically, even that doesn't change the peaceful look across her face. "You need to wake up! I NEED YOU TO WAKE UP!" My eyes don't leave Gram's face while I blindly reach for the phone on the table next to her bed. Pill bottles rattle as they hit the floor. Something glass shatters at my feet. At last, I reach the phone and dial those three dreadful numbers.

Through my sobs, I try to explain to the emergency operator what's going on. Dad coughs and my breath catches when my eye's meet his. His eyes are blood shot and he's crying. This is the first time in my whole life that I have seen him cry. I try hard to listen to what she's instructing me to do but I can't focus, not now.

"Ma'am, did you hear me? I need you to lay her flat on the floor so that I can walk you through CPR. The ambulance is on its way."

It took the ambulance thirty minutes to leave. With each minute that ticked by, and every sympathetic look the EMT's gave us, what I already knew was confirmed. Gram passed away. My best friend is *gone*.

I swear anyone and everyone has stopped by today. After the eighth unwelcomed hug, I locked myself in my room. I just want people to stop touching me. The only person I need a hug from and to tell me everything will be okay, can't.

If one more person asks me if I want to go to the funeral home to see her body one last time before they cremate her, I'm going to lose it more than I already have. No, I don't want to see my best friends' lifeless body as it discolors. I want to remember her as peaceful as she looked this morning.

I don't want the familiar scent that is Gram to be replaced or tainted with the sterile hospital scent. I want to remember the way Gram has always smelled of cucumber melon body spray and Juicy Fruit.

I don't want to remember her being draped in some cloth that has probably covered hundreds of bodies. I want to remember her wearing a white t-shirt and jeans with the elastic around her ankles.

I just want to remember my Gram the way she deserves, just the way she was. Is that too much to ask for?

Over and over, I've replayed last night's dream. Was that some sort of way for Gram to say goodbye? I know she didn't believe in goodbyes because goodbyes are forever, but that's what this is, right? Goodbye?

Someone knocks lightly and I wipe the tears away even though no one is coming in.

"Emma, sweetie. Will you please open up for auntie?" Aunt Karen begs from the other side of my bedroom door.

"I'll be down in a bit." I say matter-of-factly.

She sobs and I begin to feel selfish for hiding out, but I just need space. If that makes me selfish then so be it. "David's making your favorite for dinner."

"I'm not hungry."

Sometimes I forget just how thin these walls are. When Aunt Karen takes a deep breath, I'm quickly reminded. "Whenever you're ready there will be a plate waiting for you."

"Thanks." Is all I manage to get out before I start crying again.

Chapter Thirty-Seven

Gram only had three wishes to follow after she passed away.

First request- To be cremated.

Second request- Sprinkle her ashes over the dump.

Third request- Absolutely no service. Instead, a cookout to celebrate her life.

We all decided that Gram will get two out of her three wishes granted. We had her cremated but there's no way we will be *sprinkling* her over the dump. We understand how much her and her lifelong friend loved dump picking, but no way.

Her third request is the reason that I have been asked for what feels like the hundredth time today where the food goes. *Probably on the table that's already overflowing with food* is what I want to say, but I just point to the table. I appreciate everyone's generosity, but I really don't want to be here around people.

● ● ●

"I'm sorry about your Gram." Someone that I don't recognize says before wrapping their arms around me, I recoil.

I'm not a people person, especially not today. And there's nothing I despise more than hugs. Why do people think it's perfectly fine to just hug people? Whatever happened to handshakes? They are effective, brief, and no one's personal space is compromised. "Thanks."

"Emma, the hotdogs just came off the grill if you're hungry." Dad says as he takes the seat next to me and I take a seat in my chair before anyone else can hug me.

"We know how much you love everything that's in a hotdog." Uncle Alan butts in sarcastically.

"I'm actually not hungry." especially now that I'm thinking about how hotdogs are made. Thanks Uncle Alan.

"Neither am I." Dad laughs, and it breaks my heart. I haven't seen him cry since the morning Gram passed away and I can see how hard he's trying to hold it together.

"What are you guys doing all the way over here?" Uncle Troy, Aunt Lori and their two kids, Liam and Tracey, pull up chairs and join us. "Everyone else is over there." He points to the crowd gathered on the other side of the yard.

"Exactly." Uncle Alan laughs his usual loud contagious laugh and within seconds, we're all laughing and crying.

Grief is a weird thing. One minute I'm on the verge of cursing someone out for simply asking where they should put another potato salad, and the next, I'm laughing and crying simultaneously. When does the rollercoaster end?

"What's going on over here?" The confused look on Marie's face is priceless as she looks at each of us. She already know our family is crazy, unlike the group across the yard that keep pointing and whispering.

Uncle Alan wipes his eyes and waves for her to pull up an empty chair. "It's good to see you sweetie."

Marie bends down with ease to give her dad a hug before pulling up her chair. "You too, Daddy."

Uncle Troy starts laughing hysterically. "Hey, remember that time up in Vermont when Mom had us paint Dad's van?"

"Jesum crow. Now there was nothing wrong with the paint! I don't know what your mother was thinking!" Ashes from Grandpa's cigar start falling in his lap, but I don't think he notices or cares.

"Dad, you're going to set yourself on fire!" Aunt Karen warns while squeezing her chair amongst us.

That does it for Dad. Tears roll down his face and he tries to say something but he's laughing too hard.

"Do you know how long it took us to paint that van?" Uncle Troy asks.

Aunt Karen starts giggling. "Oh, are you guys talking about that light green van? Dad, Mom just wanted to surprise you!"

"Yeah, well I was surprised alright!" This must be why Grandpa never seems to be a fan of surprises. By the sounds of it, I wouldn't like them either after that.

"You wouldn't even drive it again until the paint was taken off!" Uncle Alan shouts between laughing spurts.

Dad takes a deep breath and gives whatever he was going to say another try. "She came out holding a bucket of forest green paint, brushes and... rollers!"

"She just wanted the door to match the rest of the van!" Uncle Troy starts crying with the rest of us.

Thankfully, everyone else is still congregated around the food. Otherwise, they may question our sanity more than they already have. But then again, we did just lose one of the biggest staples in our dysfunctional family. If people think we belong in a padded room, so be it.

"I remember for my twelfth birthday; Mom threw me a surprise party with all of my girlfriends. She played it off that I wasn't having a party, so well, that I believed her. There was even a purple Barbie doll cake. To this day, that's still my favorite birthday."

"Hey, I remember Gram having a few Barbie cakes for Emmy and me too!" Marie adds.

"Remember that year for Halloween when she dressed up like a black cat?" This was by far the coolest Halloween I can remember.

"Yes! And we were Pocahontas? Dad, remember that year?"

"Of course, sweetie. We loved taking you kids trick or treating! That year, your mother and I dressed up as pirates."

Aunt Karen straightens. "I think I have a picture of that Halloween. I will have to look for it."

As Aunt Karen mentions it, visions of her mail and pictures drifting to the barn floor when I rummaged through her hutch come to mind. It feels like more than a month since I have been in the barn. I wonder if she has also met Gustavo. She must have. I already know she can see what I can, and she has been in the barn many times.

Chapter Thirty-Eight

As I lay here staring at the chipping paint on my bedroom ceiling, my phone rings for the fifty-third time in three days. And yet again, I choose to let it ring. I have no desire to talk to anyone. There's nothing else anyone could say to make the pain lessen. Part of me is also waiting to see if Gram comes back to haunt me like she promised during my preteen attitude phase. As much as I wish to see her just one more time, I seriously hope that she was able to find peace and move on. I think finding out that she is stuck in this house with the *others* would destroy what little faith I have left.

Gram deserves peace.

My phone starts ringing again, making me jump. Without bothering to see who it is, I toss it to the other end of my bed. When will people take the hint?

"Hey you!" Collin shouts as he barges through my bedroom door, causing a few flakes of paint to float to the floor.

● ● ●

The room spins from sitting up too fast and I brace myself until it finally slows. That's what I get for not eating the last week. "What are you doing here?"

"Well," He crosses his arms across his chest, "I've been trying to get ahold of you for three days now."

"Is everything alright?" I guess I probably could have at least read a few of the texts.

"That's why I came over. You tell me."

"I don't really want to talk about it."

"Fine. Get up and get ready." He pulls my hands but I'm too stubborn to stand.

"Ready for what?" I don't have anywhere to be today, that's why I'm still in my pjs.

"A party. I have someone that I want you to meet." His eyebrow wiggles, making me almost laugh.

"Oh no. I'm not going to a party. My Gram passed away."

"I'm sorry to hear that." He says sympathetically while sitting down next to me. "Wanna talk about it?"

I shake my head and he stands.

"Alright then, get up! Let's go!"

"Dude, I need to shower, and I don't even know if I have anything to wear."

"Emma, you have an overflowing dresser right there. Grab some clothes and go get ready. I'll wait. As your friend, I can't let you sit in this room for another day by yourself." He's got a good point. If this were a couple months ago, I would have begged to leave.

"Who's your friend?" Not that I'm interested in dating anyone, but maybe getting out would do me some good. Afterall, I can't stay here forever, and I definitely don't want to.

"His name is Michael. He skateboards, plays guitar, wicked funny, great at beer pong and if I were a girl, I would…"

"Okay! Alright, Give me about fifteen minutes?"

"Yep."

My dresser may be overflowing but those are mainly clothes that are too small. Since the last time I ate was with Gram, about a week ago, something in here should fit now.

The numbness that has consumed my body makes it easier to walk past the creepy room hallway. At this point, if they wanted to take me out, I'd probably let them. Fortunately, they are trapped. I can still hear the voices almost all of the time but at least I don't have to see them.

"Dammit Mom! Stop shutting the T.V off!" Dad shouts out of frustration as I reach the living room.

"Dad, what's going on?"

"Your grandmother is haunting me. The damn T.V keeps shutting off. I know it's her, Emma."

I laugh a little. "Dad, I think you just need a new T.V. If Gram we're here, I'd sense her." Right? Surely, I would notice. What if I'm just too numb to feel her presence? No, that can't be it. Gram might have been restless most of her life, but she looked at peace.

Chapter Thirty-Nine

Present Day

"Help me!" Abigail shouts and I run down the narrow hallway as fast as I can. Before I can reach her, the door slams shut and she lets out a blood curdling scream.

"No! Don't hurt her!" clenching my fist, I bang on the door until blood is dripping down my arms.

My body jolts awake. I'm drenched in sweat and when I realize it was just another nightmare, I wait for my breathing to slow before climbing out of bed. Michael stirs beside me but doesn't wake up. During the twenty years that we have been together, he has witnessed many of my nightmares, but I still feel bad every time that I wake him. Luckily, the worst of the nightmares only happen once a week or so.

Over the last nineteen years I have tried to erase everything associated with the gray house. Good and bad.

Countless therapists have tried their best and medications only heightened my anxiety, making it almost unbearable.

Our house is dark and silent as I get out of bed. I wait until I'm in the kitchen to see what time it is since I already know it's around four in the morning. The nightmares always happen at exactly the same time. Sure enough, the clock on the stove confirms that it is exactly four. I sigh and begin my morning routine while our two cats, Twinkle Toes and Cat Boy try to trip me. They must be the most impatient cats ever. Ignoring them for a minute while I start some coffee only entices them further. Once they have their breakfast, they leave me alone and I'm free to sit in the quiet while I sip my first cup of coffee of the day. I'm not sure when I started liking coffee, but Gram and Grandpa were right.

Back in my teenage years, I never thought I would be able to enjoy the quiet. For the longest time, I didn't think such a thing could exist. That was until Michael and I bought our house. At first glance, we didn't think the blue house hidden behind trees and gigantic bushes would be the house for us. But once we stepped inside, we were sold. It was quiet, actually quiet. No restless spirits, no loud neighbors, no heavy traffic. Just silence. That was the first time in years that I felt at peace. Ever since then, this has been my safe haven. Even though the nightmares continue, I'm able to sleep knowing that our three boys will never have to experience anything like I did growing up in the gray house.

Our bedroom door creaks open and when I turn around, Michael is walking towards where I'm sitting on the couch. He rubs the sleep out of his eyes before pulling me in for a hug and a morning kiss. Michael and our kids are the only people that I can stand touching me. Somedays, I'll admit I can't handle it, but it's getting easier.

"What time did you wake up?" He whispers. I love that he too, enjoys the peace and quiet.

"Four. Coffee is ready." I smile and follow him into the kitchen. I wince when I see the clock reveals it's almost six. "I'll make some fresh coffee." Time never fails to slip by during the early peaceful hours.

Before I can dump out the now cold coffee, he pours half a cup and smiles. "Thank you."

While the coffee is brewing, I start a load of laundry and begin making the boys lunches for school.

"Are you going grocery shopping today?" Michael asks just before wrapping his arms around me. His grip loosens as he feels my body tense, but I pull his arms tighter. Michael is my comfort and after that nightmare, I need this. I need him.

"Yeah, is there anything that you would like?" I inhale slowly and lean my head back on his chest. Moments like this are what help push the past back further in my mind.

"Maybe just some of that black bean salsa, if they have it." Playfully, he tickles my side and I laugh. Even though he does this often, almost every time I'm caught off guard.

"I'll check. Just write it down so I don't forget." Not that that brings much relief because more than half the time, I end up forgetting the list or half the items on it anyways.

"Mom! Do we have tin foil, paper clips, wire and tape?" James, our oldest, shouts throughout the house. I can only imagine what he needs all of that for.

"Oops, I think we woke the kids up." Michael whispers.

"Shh. James, you're going to wake up your brothers." I know they will be waking up any minute but who doesn't enjoy just a few more minutes of calmness?

"But I just need this stuff for my project." He defends while shuffling through the junk drawer, also known as his treasure chest. Ever since he was three, he has been making projects out of meaningless trash. Now, at thirteen, he's made some incredible projects and has won first place in every science fair that he has entered for the last five years.

"Mommy! Are the muffins ready?" Daniel whines from his bedroom downstairs and Michael and I start laughing. Daniel has always loved his food. I'm not sure where these boys put it all. At nine, Daniel is almost as tall as me but still a beanpole, just like his brothers.

"Come up here and you'll find out." Michael shouts down the stairs.

"Ugh! No yelling!" I can't help but laugh at Peter. He is always loud, but apparently, he is the only one that can be. Eleven-year-olds are so moody.

After the typical morning chaos, everyone is in the car and ready to go to school.

I roll down my window for one more kiss from Michael before we all head out. "Have a great Friday! I love you, Michael."

"I love you too!" Before getting into his truck, he pulls my door open. Just as his lips meet mine, for a moment, any concern or unnerving feeling vanishes. That is, until the choir begins.

"Come on, guys! I don't want to be late!" James whines and I find this extremely ironic considering he is the reason we are late most of the time.

"Eww! That's disgusting!"

"Just wait a few more years, Peter." Michael laughs and I roll my eyes. I'm not ready for the teenage years. Can we just go back to when they just wanted to talk about Minecraft all day, every day?

"Can we stop for a second breakfast?"

"James, you will not be late. Daniel, you already had breakfast and you have a lunchbox full of snacks." Reaching into my snack stash, that I've always kept in my car because I never know when these boys are going to be *starving,* I pull out a granola bar and toss it behind me.

At last, we are backing out of the driveway and on our way to the bus stop at the bottom of our hill. Unhurriedly, I put the car in park. Drop off is my least favorite part of the day. Especially on days like today. Something feels wrong.

"Alright James, I hope you have a great Friday. I love you."

"I love you too, Mom." Since we are the first ones here, he leans over and gives me a hug. I squeeze him as hard as I can and kiss the top of his head, just like my Gram used to do, before finally letting him go.

I fight back the tears that are stinging my eyes as he gets out of the car. I hate days like this. Usually, my mornings are a little off after a nightmare but for whatever reason, I can't shake this eerie feeling.

Another car parks behind us and I get out to hug Peter and Daniel. Thankfully, they are not too cool for Mom yet. "I'll see you guys after school! I love you!" The bus screeches to a stop, and all I get is a quick wave as they take their seats and the bus drives away.

Flicking through the radio presets, I hope to find anything that's not the news. During the third pass, one of the ninety's stations promises to play a song after this advertisement. Since the other ones haven't even started on the weather, I decide to wait it out.

Sure enough, the song that starts playing through the speakers is crap.

"Spotify it is."

Some people have multiple playlists, not me though. I just have one playlist that I have been adding songs to for the last fifteen years. It's always a surprise as to what song will play next since it's such a wide variety. Taylor Swift is the first. For a brief moment my mind drifts back to the party where Michael and I met. We talked about anything and everything until the sun came up and he had to go to work. That will forever be one of my favorite nights.

The next song interrupts my thoughts, "Have you ever felt pain so powerful, so heavy you collapse. No, well..." Screw this band and their apparent perfect life. Next.

"I close my eyes when I get too sad. I think thoughts that I know are bad. Close my eyes and I count to ten. Hope it's over when I open them." Alright, I'll let this one play out. It's too bad Everclear didn't come out with this song back in my teens. My teenage self could have used it.

Finally, I'm at the coffee shop, which means my day should begin turning around. This also means that I'm halfway to the grocery store. After waiting for what feels like forever, I'm handed my coffee. This coffee shop is always a hit or miss, so I'm impressed with how great it tastes. It's a relief because I definitely need extra coffee today.

I stop at the red light by the convenience store and take a deep breath. Nineteen years have passed since we had the gray house condemned but it doesn't stop me from looking for Gram in the living room windows every time I drive by.

The closer I get, I slow down.

Gram's face is clear as day in the middle window. It breaks my heart that she is trapped there. I so badly wish I knew how to find her peace so that she can move on.

A few years ago, I contacted a paranormal investigating team. They went in several times and each time they found something more disturbing than the last. While reviewing their findings, I heard someone warning them to get out. I have no doubt that was Gram. I think she's only staying there to protect anyone else from being consumed by *him*. They asked a few times if I would go with them, every time my answer was no. Even with Gram being there, I couldn't do it.

Chapter Forty

By the time I get out of the grocery store, I still can't shake this uneasy feeling. Maybe I'll see if Esther wants to come over for coffee. While I wait for her to message me back, I'll call Marie. She's always good at talking me down from feeling like this.

After a few rings she answers. "Hey." She says sleepily.

"Crap, did I wake you up?" Marie has never been an early riser like me. Just as I've never been a night owl like her, with the exception of my teenage years and the years of insomnia that followed.

"Yeah, but it's fine. I need to get up anyways. Are you driving? It sounds like you're driving."

"I just went grocery shopping."

"I don't know how you are always up so early!"

"Years of trauma and nightmares will have that effect."

"I'm sorry, Emma. What was last nights about?"

There are very few that I go into detail explaining to anyone. This time is not one of them. "I wish I could have helped them, Marie."

I hear her let out a deep breath. "I know you do; I know."

"Usually, I can shake the feeling but for some reason today I can't."

"Have you passed *it* yet? I know it adds a solid half hour to your drive home, but maybe you should take the other way home, so you don't have to see it again today."

"Eh. Too late, I'm already heading that way. I saw Gram on my way to the store."

"I can't believe she's still there. But what's more unbelievable is that house *still* being there. How has it not collapsed yet?"

"What in the world..." From up the street, I can see construction vehicles now surrounding the gray house. They weren't there the first time I drove by.

"Emma? Emma, what's going on?"

"I... I'll call you back." I say before tossing my phone in the passenger seat.

Tunnel vision kicks in and all I can see it the gray house. Horns honk around me, letting me know that I ran the last red light. Traffic cones are blocking off the lane directly in front of the house. Impulsively, I park in front of the first cone and walk towards the house.

Are they really tearing this house down? Finally? After we had it condemned, they found out that they can't build any further back because of the flood zone. Gram was right. They were also told that they can't build anything else in its place. So, with no use for the property, they just let it cave in.

Maybe now there will be peace. Not only for myself, but also for the many others, living and nonliving, that have had their lives altered by this dwelling.

I was beginning to think this day would never come. The rumble of bulldozers and dump trucks that reverberate down the busy street. Peering at the immense gray shell in front of me, a shiver runs down my spine. If this is supposed to bring me peace, then why do I feel so apprehensive?

The roar of the first bulldozer is deafening as the bucket raises and takes a chunk of the decrepit roof. The hundreds of pigeons, that have made nests throughout the plaster covered wood lath walls, fly out in flocks.

As hard as I try not to glance at the tiny window above the front porch, my eyes deceive me and shift anyways. In that tiny window, Abby stands alone, in the familiar dirty and ripped white dress. Just as I somehow knew she would be. The scared and sad expression that she usually wears on her child-like face has been replaced with something dark. The blackened eyes and grin that has preempted the once was angel face, let's me know that *he* is here. *He* will always be here.

I despise this place and just about everything associated with it. I always will.

As the second bulldozer lifts towards the roof of the attached barn, the long-standing wood crumbles, leaving behind a cloud of dust. Amongst the pile of ruins, something catches my eye, it's a blue and gray Power Wheels motorcycle that once belonged to my little brother Jake. Memories of the day we moved in flood my thoughts. That is until the nightmares from the past twenty something years come crashing down.

My eyes drift once more until I see Gram. Only she doesn't look the same. Her face resembles a skeleton, and I can only imagine the toll this place has taken on her, even after her death.

"Hey! You can't go in there!" A man shouts from behind me and I stop as my hand grazes the front doorknob.

What am I doing? He's right, I can't go in there.

But I just need to tell Gram how much I miss her one last time. I hope this brings her the peace that she deserves. She has always made it her mission to protect everyone. Now it's time for her to join Grandpa and Uncle Alan and rest peacefully.

The cool metal turns in my palm and everything goes black.

"I told you that you would be back." The familiar voice from my nightmare's hiss and I gasp. "Now you are going down with the rest of us."

Gradually, my vision returns, and my chest tightens as I peer around at the disintegrating walls covered in black mold. A chunk is missing from the roof but somehow the four-pane window has remained intact. "No! This cannot be real! I must be having a nightmare."

"This is a nightmare alright. Just one that you're not going to wake up from." He growls.

Frantically, I jump to my feet but there's nowhere for me to go. The floor of the creepy room has given out from years of neglect, save for the little section of floor that I'm standing on, directly under the little window. The rumbling of the equipment quiets and I bang my fist against the window as hard as I can.

"HELP ME!"

"I'm sorry, Emma." Abigail cries.

"I warned you all those years ago not to come back." Gustavo defends.

"I LET YOU ALL BE. I LET THIS HOUSE BE! I HAD IT CONDEMED SO THAT YOU COULD ALL CONTINUE YOUR SICK REVENGE ON EACHOTHER WITHOUT HARMING ANYONE ELSE. LEAVE ME THE FUCK ALONE!"

"EMMA!" Gram's raspy voice breaks through my panic. "Emma, look at Grammy!"

This is the first time I have been this close to Gram since that morning she passed away. Ironically, she feels just as cold as that morning. I miss this woman more than anything. Even though she's directly in front of me, I still can't hug her. Tears stream down my face. What was I thinking stopping here? I should have turned around and taken the long way home like Marie suggested.

I have to look away when Gram starts talking. This is not how I want to remember Gram looking. "I will make sure you get out of here. You don't belong here. Now is not your time, Emma."

He snickers. "That's where you're wrong, Rose."

"I'm never wrong, Darius. I will always protect my family. It all comes to an end today."

Acknowledgements

To say this book has been emotionally draining wouldn't scratch the surface of the toll it took to complete it. I did it though, thanks to many amazing people, sleepless nights, horrific nightmares, 603 Seltzers, and far too much coffee. I tried to put my thanks in order, but no matter how many times I rearrange the list, it seems unfair. So instead, I'm just going to list this randomly since everyone has had a pretty even contribution. Besides my gram, she gets the spotlight first and intentionally. It's the least I could do.

Gram. You aren't here to read this, but if you were, I know you would read it a thousand times over. Out of 59,903 words, chapter thirty-six was the most difficult to write. So difficult that I had a mental break down and a two-week long panic attack just from the anticipation leading up to it and had to take a break from writing. Not only was I dreading writing about your death, but also reliving the day my whole world crashed. Then one day I decided that it might actually do my mental health some good to write it down. Not even halfway through the first line of chapter thirty-six, tears started trickling on the keyboard. I'm surprised my laptop didn't short out from water damage by the end of that chapter. There isn't a day that passes that I don't miss you more. Almost sixteen years with you was not enough.

My husband. We met during my lowest and darkest days. Every day since then, you've inspired me to be a better person. As much as I appreciate you being home to help with the boys at night now, I appreciate not feeling scared of my own shadow while home alone with the boys after working on this book more. Thank you for EVERYTHING.

Jess. Eventually I will be inspired to finish the follow up book to The Gray House, I promise. I can feel it manifesting. Until then, be prepared to be dragged out of your comfort zone because I'm going to need your opinions on my *other* books. You were my first beta reader and if it wasn't for your constant begging, I mean *motivational pushing* for me to finish the next chapter, we both know I wouldn't have finished it. Thank you for letting me pay you in coffee.

Uncle Iver. When I asked you what you thought of me writing this, you said I should go for it. When I asked what you had thought about it so far, you said you weren't reading it until it was a paperback. I was a little hurt, but I can't blame you, who doesn't like reading actual books? Plus, that gave me the push I needed to not give up on getting published, even if I have to self-publish. Thank you for that.

Pam Brooks Crowley. Thank you for reaching out to me after I shared my story to show me the incredible picture you captured of The Gray House. I owe you an even bigger thank you for allowing me to use it as the cover of this book. You are an amazing photographer, and I am always in awe of your work.

● ● ●

Black River Paranormal. Leanne, Alaura and Kayla are three of the bravest women I know. When I first contacted you, I had very little knowledge on how to get in contact with the property owner, but you went above and beyond for this investigation. Thank you for risking your lives to fulfill my picture requests. I look forward to working with you ladies for future books. (If anyone is interested in seeing that investigation or pictures, go check out their Facebook page!)

Sidney. Things were far from easy back then but I'm glad I always had you by my side, literally. We may live our separate lives now, but we always pick up right where we left off. Well not exactly where we left off, each time is better than before. I can't wait to see what your future holds. Keep me updated when you have a chance, even if you have to randomly drop by because you lost my number. Actually, that's not a bad idea, maybe then we can take that yearly photo we both know is way past due.

Dad. You may not have been the greatest listener during my teenage years, but I was also a handful. Thank you for always being there no matter what.

Shannon. On behalf of everyone who has read this or plan to, thank you for correcting my many grammatical errors. I know this isn't your preferred genre but don't worry, I have plenty more coming your way that will be!

Heidi. Thank you for our coffee date. Hearing your experiences made me feel at ease, even though I had goosebumps almost the entire two/three-ish hours. Let's get together soon.

* * *

Aunt Jen and Eric. I'm still frustrated that I gave up my room. Had I not, I never would have moved upstairs, and this book wouldn't exist. So, thanks?

Everyone who knew me back in my teens. I feel like I should apologize for the person I was back then. I'm not going to though. Those actions were those of a troubled and angry teenage girl. That troubled angry girl no longer exists and if she did, she wouldn't deserve your forgiveness.

Finally, everyone who has read this story. I will always be thankful for all of you. I enjoy hearing and reading your experiences. No matter how crazy you think you may sound, please know that I don't think you're crazy at all. So please continue sharing!

Made in the USA
Middletown, DE
11 December 2022

16728482R00170